LEGAL EAGLES

Tom Logan has a law partner who put a dog on the witness stand.
A client who cannot enter a room without a crime being committed.
And a case that could turn out to be the murder of the year. His.

ROBERT REDFORD
DEBRA WINGER   DARYL HANNAH

An IVAN REITMAN Film

LEGAL EAGLES

A NEW COMEDY FROM THE DIRECTOR OF GHOSTBUSTERS

BRIAN DENNEHY   TERENCE STAMP   STEVEN HILL

Screenplay by JIM CASH & JACK EPPS, JR.
Story by IVAN REITMAN & JIM CASH & JACK EPPS, JR.
Music by ELMER BERNSTEIN
Production Design by JOHN DE CUIR
Director of Photography LASZLO KOVACS, A.S.C.
Executive Producers JOE MEDJUCK and MICHAEL C. GROSS
Produced and Directed by IVAN REITMAN

LEGAL EAGLES

Novel by Martin Owens
Based on a story by Ivan Reitman &
Jim Cash & Jack Epps, Jr.
Screenplay by Jim Cash & Jack Epps, Jr.

Library of Congress Catalog Card Number: 86-45563

ISBN 0-918432-74-X

LEGAL EAGLES was set in a version of Garamond. Typesetting was
done by Crane Typesetting Services, Inc. The book was printed and
bound by Maple-Vail Book Manufacturing Group.

New York Zoetrope
80 East 11th Street
New York, NY 10003

Printed in the United States of America
First Printing: May, 1986
5 4 3 2 1

LEGAL EAGLES

A NOVEL BY MARTIN OWENS

BASED ON A STORY BY
IVAN REITMAN & JIM CASH & JACK EPPS, JR.
SCREENPLAY BY
JIM CASH & JACK EPPS, JR.

Prologue

Chelsea's father had said it would be the grooviest birthday party ever. It was August fifth, nineten sixty-eight. Chelsea Deardon was eight years old and still having birthday parties, and people were still saying "groovy." Her father had decided the party would be held in his studio, which was a room in their home on West Tenth Street in Manhattan, in the heart of the artists' district.

Their place was a converted bank. On one side, the tellers' cages had been left to partition off the kitchen. The cages were used by people in the kitchen to pass food through to the long rustic table on the other side. The vault door had been retained, as well; it opened to reveal a cot and bookshelves. Her father loved the absurdity of the setting: it was the perfect place for a sixties artist to live, the perfect statement for him to make. When she thought about it years later, Chelsea decided it wasn't so absurd; a bank was the perfect place for it all to begin.

But that night she hadn't worried about symbols; she hadn't worried about anything. She had just been enthralled by the gaiety of the party, by the fuss, by the food, the loud music—all for her. She looked up and took it in, awestruck: the huge white walls rising painted to a height of twelve feet; the giant bronze chandelier, hanging twinkling in the center of the ceiling, with stainless steel bullet-shaped floodlights as its candles; the chrome and green leatherette chairs around the table. The idea, her father had tried to explain, was to clash styles. But all she saw that night were grandeur and fun.

Grandeur and fun and people. Colorful, iconoclastic, counterculture people: some wearing antique Chinese robes, others miniskirts; some wearing suits, others jeans; some men with hair as long as her own waist-length blonde hair, others with hair cropped close to their heads. Laughing, singing, drinking, smoking—especially smoking, all types of things.

There were famous people there, too, though Chelsea hadn't known they were famous at the time. She knew one only as "Uncle Bill" (de Kooning), another as "Uncle Roy" (Lichtenstein); or that funny one, "Uncle Andy," running around telling people they would all be famous for fifteen minutes. (Her father said there was no time limit for being infamous, so he was safe.) They had all brought her the loveliest—and in some cases, the weirdest—presents, everything from dresses to mobiles to dartboards of President Johnson.

Her father, of course, had given her the greatest gift of all. He had shushed the crowd and called for the loud acid rock to be stilled. Then he had lifted her up in his arms.

She could still remember exactly what he was wearing: beige corduroy pants, a bluejean shirt and a burgundy knit tie. His hands smelled faintly, as they always did, of turpentine. His face was still slightly stubbly, for he shaved absent-mindedly, as he did most everything but paint.

Before the quieted crowd, he had kissed her small, round, cherubic face. He had announced that she was pretty as a picture, hip to the joke of the cliche; "pretty" wasn't what most critics called his pictures. "Pretentious," "inaccessible," "vibrant," "imaginative"—these were more likely to be the adjectives used to describe his controversial work. Dozens of his canvases now stood stacked around the place, facing the walls.

Then he had winked at someone she couldn't see, and a second later, the biggest, most beautiful cake in the world was wheeled forward. A gasp of pleasure went up from the crowd. Chelsea was too thrilled to make a sound; mute, she only opened her mouth, stunned by the joy of such a sight. Then Sebastian Deardon, the controversial rebel painter, led his jaded, stoned and famous friends in a sincere off-key chorus of "Happy Birthday."

When they had finished, Chelsea was giggling helplessly with delight. Sebastian had let her down—she would have gladly stayed in his arms forever—and she had waved and curtseyed to the applauding crowd.

Sebastian spoke then. "I want to thank all you freeloaders for helping me celebrate Chelsea's eighth birthday. I'm the proudest father in the world. No one's got a more talented kid. Her paintings are already better than mine."

There was more laughter and applause; Deardon waited for it to end.

"So, for her birthday, Chelsea and I have decided to trade art. She is giving me this wonderful painting of hers and I am giving her this modest but original Sebastian Deardon."

On cue, Chelsea held up a little plastic plate on which she had painted a landscape. The crowd made a great show of appreciation.

"Wonderful!" they cried. "Beautiful! Groovy!"

After his daughter had gotten her first taste of critical acclaim, Deardon produced a painting he had taken from a stack behind him. He handed it as a gift to his daughter.

Chelsea took the unframed abstract work into her hands. She did

9

not understand it, of course; there were plenty of people four times her age who didn't. But she had an opinion on it just the same.

"Oh, Daddy," she said. "I love it."

Smiling, Sebastian bent near her. He gently took the picture from her hands. Then with a piece of charcoal, he wrote, very gingerly, on its back:

"To Chelsea, my favorite artist—Sebastian Deardon."

He handed it back and Chelsea hugged the painting to her chest. The guests gave a last, touched burst of applause and cheers.

Then Deardon kissed his daughter and whispered in her ear,

"One piece of cake and then Nanny will tuck you in."

In her memory Nanny's face was hazy but her hand was still warm. She steered Chelsea to the cake table, as the party turned loud again. Still clutching her gift, Chelsea ate the cake; then Nanny led her from the party itself.

On the brink of leaving, she turned to take one last look, to make it last a minute longer. She saw that her father was now talking to two men, both slim and elegant. He was no longer smiling; instead he seemed angry. Chelsea did not know what he was angry about but she knew the two men's names: Victor Taft and Robert Forrester.

Chelsea put her father's angry face from her mind. She lay in bed remembering only the pleasure of the party and the people—and her painting. She placed it carefully on the table beside her bed.

Nanny kissed her forehead and then left her side. She put out the light and closed the door. Chelsea was in the dark with only her painting as company. The faint noises of the party grew fainter. She fell asleep, smiling.

She did not know how long she slept. She only knew that she was awakened, suddenly, and not by Nanny. A light from the hall shone into her face but it seemed filtered, diffused, by something

10

in the air. It was only when she took a breath that she realized it was smoke.

She was being scooped up and carried in a man's arms. The man was not her father. It was, she realized, as she managed to open her eyes, Victor Taft: one of the men who had made her father mad.

He tried to take her immediately from the room but Chelsea slowed him down. Instinctively, her arm reached out for the painting by her bed. But her fingers found nothing. The painting was gone.

"Quickly, Chelsea," Taft shouted at her, "there's no time! Let's go!"

She was whisked away. Taft carried her into the apartment corridor, which was steaming hot, smoke-infested and filled with fire. Along with her senses of sight and sound, her hearing returned then. She took in the fast approaching wails of fire engines. She felt a groggy panic; her lungs felt blocked. She began to cough, then hack. Taft shielded her face with his jacket.

Taft paused then to open a door. Chelsea pushed a corner of his jacket aside and looked in; it was her father's studio.

Even through the smoke, she could see the burgundy of her father's tie; he was lying motionless on the floor. Robert Forrester, her father's other opponent that evening, stood there looking down at him. His face trembled slightly. Flames surrounded them.

Forrester turned and caught sight of Taft and the child.

"For Christ's sake, Bob!" Taft shouted, suddenly. "Get the hell out of there!"

Chelsea was shrieking then, her arms reaching out helplessly, the way she had reached for her painting, as if she could grab and carry her father.

"Daddy!" she cried.

It was too late. Taft was dragging her back down the corridor again. Soon Forrester caught up to them, coughing, his coat singed.

Behind them, the ceiling beams slowly started to snap in the studio, leaving the ceiling unsupported. Within a second, the ceiling itself had crashed to the floor, covering all that lay there.

As the three of them fled through the door of the building, Chelsea could not see for her tears. All she saw were her father's face and her father's painting; all she heard were sirens and screams she soon realized were her own.

Chapter One

Tom Logan thought he smelled smoke.

He couldn't be sure, but his senses did not often deceive him. An Assistant District Attorney had to be able to trust his hunches, and Logan usually did and was usually right; that was why at forty-four, he was rumored to be in line for the top job of D.A.

Today, however, was not a murder trial or a kidnapping case; it was a day with his daughter, something to which he always looked forward and which he always treasured. Relaxing his prosecutorial instincts, he soon forgot his suspicions. He stopped sniffing; he turned his attention back to the TV.

Maybe it had only been the power of suggestion, anyway; the news was showing black-and-white footage of a burning building, circa nineteen sixty-eight.

"This was the scene eighteen years ago," the reporter was saying, "as millions of dollars worth of Sebastian Deardon paintings literally went up in smoke above the skyline of Manhattan. Deardon himself perished in the flames, trapped inside his blazing studio. Surviving the inferno was his eight-year-old daughter, Chelsea."

Now the footage became contemporary and was in color. A Manhattan precinct station was shown. A lithe and beautiful blond woman in her twenties was led handcuffed by police through the door. Reporters were hounding her, both with questions and with equipment. Slowly, reluctantly, she turned her face to the camera.

She looked disoriented and helpless, yet a sensuousness still emanated from her piercing blue eyes and her full lips. She appeared confused yet defiant, like a cornered animal determined to survive. Logan could not help feeling that she was looking straight at him.

It was not as silly as it seemed. Chelsea Deardon was going to be his next case.

"Last night," the reporter continued, "the same Chelsea Deardon was arrested for attempting to steal one of her deceased father's paintings from the Manhattan penthouse of developer Robert Forrester. Police apprehended her several blocks from the scene after . . ."

Suddenly, Chelsea disappeared. She was replaced first by Mr. Rogers ("Can you say . . .") then by Bob Barker ("Come on down!") and then by MTV (lyrics unintelligible). Wincing, Logan turned.

"Hey," he said. "I was watching that."

He did not say it with anger. He said it with the bemusement of a father whose child was growing beyond his grasp, of a man living alone and looking for a way to cope. And these things were exactly what Tom Logan was.

"Hey," he said again. "I was watching that."

His daughter, Jennifer, age twelve, stood frowning cutely, holding the remote control.

"Sorry," she said, "but the news is so boring."

She had the light coloring of her father, the competent look of her mother. Logan watched her as with one surprisingly strong push, she closed the fold-out couch on which she had slept. He felt guilty about the meager sleeping arrangements. Then he looked around his two-room apartment and felt even worse.

There wasn't much furniture and what there was didn't match.

All kinds of eclectic possessions were piled up together: pots, pans, legal briefs, knick-knacks. His shelves held stacks of unorganized books, still unsorted, still unalphabetized. His stereo was hooked up lazily, the wires dangling limply in the open, the albums sitting in unsettled mounds. His laundry had been left rumpled and dirty in the corner.

Logan himself was a handsome man with dusty blond hair, a craggy face and a lean, muscular build. But he looked today like those clothes: waiting to be cleaned, pressed and made presentable. It was apparent that like his year-old bachelor pad, he needed work.

He smelled smoke again, but he decided to ignore it.

"So," he said, "packed your things?"

"Yes," Jennifer answered.

Logan searched for another parental thing to say. "Brush your teeth?"

"Yes."

Brushing teeth was good. What else? "How about your home-work?"

"Just finishing it."

Here was an ideal opportunity to exercise some discipline. Logan grew stern. "Your mother always tells me to make sure you do your homework and you always tell me you have no homework. Till minutes before you have to leave. Why is that?"

Jennifer only shrugged. "I only have to write one paragraph. On an emotion. It's easy. Can we go out for breakfast?"

"We ate out last night. When you stay with me, we're a family. We eat in. Occasionally." Logan could feel the false hearty conviction weighing down his words. "What kind of emotion?"

"Bliss."

"Bliss!" What kind of a school was she attending? Logan didn't know anything about bliss; how could she? "What do you know about bliss?"

"It's just about being happy. Right?"

"Right." Logan sighed. He did not think he could help her much on this assignment.

Jennifer looked at him suspiciously and then changed the subject. "You didn't sleep again, did you?"

"I slept." He thought perhaps the craters beneath his eyes said otherwise.

"Well, I woke up and I heard these strange sounds and—were you dancing in the bathroom?"

Logan suddenly became evasive; he felt like a suspect on the witness stand before a young female version of himself. "Dancing in the bathroom?"

"Mom said whenever you can't sleep, you tap dance in the bathroom."

Logan cursed to himself; this D.A. had a pretty good source. Sometimes during one of his frequent bouts with insomnia, he did like to secretly attempt a little Astaire or Kelly in the toilet, to tap away his legal troubles, to be somebody more carefree than an Assistant D.A. After all, his life was more than just law books and summations, no matter what his ex-wife had said to him before she left. Still, he stonewalled.

"Do you believe that?" he asked, incredulously.

Jennifer just stared silently, doggedly. The kid's technique was slick, he thought; she was wearing him down.

"Well, maybe I danced once or twice," he said. "I certainly didn't tap dance."

Jennifer wouldn't stop staring; he felt he might break down, weeping, admitting it, if she did not stop. But suddenly something diverted her.

"Do you smell something burning?" she asked.

Logan's head snapped towards the kitchen. "What?"

"Dad, the oven's on fire!"

Both of them ran into the kitchen. There black smoke was billowing out of the oven, while a pot of oatmeal bubbled frantically on the stove.

Logan stood and looked at it. He had forgotten all about it. He thought his cooking needed work, too. Still, his senses were still intact, that was something.

"I'm on top of it . . . don't worry . . ."

He made a few decisive-looking movements towards the blaze, which somehow did not put it out. Jennifer was jumping up and down, desperately.

"I'm on top of it . . . don't worry . . ."

"You keep saying that! I'm worried!"

Finally, when it was clear that good intentions, agile feinting and hand flailing were not going to work, Logan opted for a last resort. He took up the pan of oatmeal, opened the stove, and heaved the whole mess inside.

The thick cereal smothered the fire like lava. It also decorated the oven in a style that could only be described as Early Drip and Goo.

Still, Jennifer was relieved. She put her head on her father's shoulder with loving forgiveness and thanks. Logan sighed. He thought: another exciting day in the life of the city's hotshot Assistant D.A.

Then outside he heard the familiar, rhythmic honking of his ex-wife's car.

Logan came out of the building holding Jennifer atop his shoulders. He carried her sleepover bag in his right hand and his briefcase in the other. He felt glad that he and Jennifer presented such an impeccable picture of Daddy and daughter—well, bliss. It made Barbara smile when she saw them; it also made her uneasy.

Barbara Jorgenson was a sleek, dark, lovely woman in her mid-thirties. She had left him to pursue her own career and perhaps to escape Logan's pursuit of his own. Now she was a fully tenured college professor with a new life, a new last name and a book she was about to write. She was safely ensconced in another existence so she was friendly with Logan but guarded; he might try to drag her back to the old one. And it had had, after all, its moments.

Logan put Jennifer down. He looked at Barbara and smiled.

"Hey," he said. "You changed your hair. It looks great."

Immediately, Barbara was suspicious of the compliment. "Why do you always say that when you know I hate my hair? My hair is my worst part."

"No," Logan said. "It's terrific, really . . ."

"Tom, break the habit. Allow me the pleasure of feeling rotten about myself, okay?"

"Your hair looks like shit," Logan said.

"Thank you."

Barbara smiled then; Logan smiled wider. This unnerved her even more, and so she moved quickly to her car.

Jennifer got into the front seat. Logan tossed her sleepover bag in the back. Barbara stuck her head in the window and kissed her daughter, as if to officially announce to Logan her return.

"Did Daddy give you breakfast?" she asked.

"Oatmeal, juice and toast. Every meal we had was perfectly balanced."

Logan winked at Jennifer. Jennifer winked back.

"I'm sure," Barbara said, with dismay.

Then she paused, seeming to prepare herself. She gave a nod of her head that signaled Logan she wished to speak to him alone.

Logan assented. The two adults moved a few paces away on the block, as Jennifer craned her head to watch them. Logan felt amused at Barbara's solemnity, but her first words wiped the smile off his face.

"Tom," she said, "about Los Angeles . . ."

"I said no," Logan responded, quickly. "It isn't open to discussion."

"Look. It's my sabbatical year. I have to research my book and there's this fabulous school in Beverly Hills . . ."

"There's this fabulous school in New York she's going to right now. Do your research here."

Logan felt himself growing angry, but he knew it was only to disguise his fright. The prospect of Jennifer thousands of miles away made him feel panicked. Who would he burn oatmeal for?

"I never thought you'd be selfish enough to deprive your daughter of a new cultural experience."

"Beverly Hills? A cultural experience?" Logan's voice became shrill. "Listen. Thanks to a half-senile judge, you have this wonderful person for twenty-six days a month. I'm not going to let you take her away the other four."

Logan turned and saw Jennifer still craning her neck at them, curiously. This broke the tension; the sight cheered him up.

"See you next week," he smiled at Barbara.

Barbara rolled her eyes and turned away from him. Logan gave another big wave to Jennifer, who waved back, with clear adoration. In a minute, Barbara had reached the car and slammed the driver's door behind her. In another minute, she had gunned out into midtown traffic.

Logan watched as they disappeared in the blur of other cars. He felt determined never to give in to Barbara; he also felt a residue of fear. When he thought of it, these were the same feelings that had seemed to come from Chelsea Deardon on the television.

Then he looked down and felt something else: like kicking himself.

He was carrying Jennifer's sleepover bag. His briefcase was in the backseat of his ex-wife's car.

Chapter Two

The Criminal Courts Building at One Hundred Centre Street in downtown Manhattan was packed that morning. As usual, there were all kinds of people from both sides of the law: cops leading cuffed suspects; lawyers prepping witnesses one last time; college interns trying to keep up with their demanding employers; and citizens with complaints trying desperately to get some attention.

There was also a man with oatmeal on his shirt carrying a pink plastic sleepover bag with a picture of Tom Petty on it.

Carol Freeman, Logan's assistant, managed to find him in the crowd. She caught up and addressed him in her usual pert and efficient way.

"Better hurry," she said. "Twenty minutes to court."

"Court?" Logan said. "This morning?"

As they walked, Freeman handed Logan a file and, not missing a step, took his bag.

"Howard Marchek—receiving stolen property." She checked out the bag in her hand. "Slumber party?"

Logan opened the file and read it, keeping up his pace. "Marchek . . . this isn't my case. It's Henning's."

He tried to hand it back to her but Freeman wouldn't receive it. "It's yours now. Henning's got laryngitis."

"He never gets sick on easy cases. This one must be tough."

Kapstan, a fellow attorney, was passing the other way. Maintaining his own swift stride, he addressed Logan without stopping.

"You were right about the landlady, Tom. I put her on the stand and she cracked like an egg. I crushed her like a walnut. She crumbled like blue cheese."

"You should open a restaurant," Logan said, as Kapstan walked on. Then he turned to Freeman. "What was he talking about?"

"Hey," Freeman said, "how'd you get oatmeal on your shirt?"

"Oatmeal?" Logan looked down. "Damn!"

They reached the door marked: THOMAS LOGAN, ASSISTANT DISTRICT ATTORNEY and passed through.

The two of them did not slow down once inside. Logan's harried, middle-aged secretary, Doreen, had to jump up if she was to catch them. She followed them from the outer office to the inner, carrying a pile of messages. The parade finally stopped there.

Logan looked at the place and felt at home, and with good reason: his office looked just like his apartment. Folders covered the desk haphazardly; casebooks were stacked on chairs, radiators, the floor. Pieces of clothing lay here and there. File cabinets were stuffed to the gills, with drawers too crammed to close. No one ever came near them; only Logan understood the system.

Doreen waved the messages at him, as if she knew this would be the first and last time today to get his attention.

"Anything important?" Logan asked her.

"Mad house," Doreen replied. "You got a call from an attorney named Whitman. He wants to plea bargain that Bedford Stuyvesant rape case."

"Tell Whitman we'll agree to put the guy back on the street if we can release him in Whitman's neighborhood."

While talking, Logan took off his tie and tossed it to Freeman, who immediately hung it around her neck. Logan began to take off his stained shirt.

"You got a new case," Freeman told him. "Puts you over the limit at fifty-two. A Chelsea Elizabeth Deardon. Attempted grand theft."

This stopped Logan, but only for a second. "Yeah. I just saw something about that on TV."

Freeman handed him the arrest report and Logan read it, quickly, as he opened a filing cabinet. From it, he removed a new shirt wrapped in cellophane.

"See if Bower's got a seat left for the Knicks tonight," he said.

"Tonight?" Freeman answered. "Tonight's the banquet, remember?"

Logan clearly did not. "Banquet?"

He was standing that way, shirtless and confused, when Blanchard entered. He had the same job as Logan but none of his style, Freeman thought, or any humor at all. He gave a look of distaste to his unkempt colleague.

"I hate to break up your aerobics class, Logan, but this is important."

"The banquet!" Logan remembered then: it was that annual affair. He was supposed to give the address. He slipped into his shirt.

Blanchard was undaunted. "I still haven't received your seven fifty form for last month."

It was as if Blanchard hadn't entered; Logan turned to Freeman. "Is my tux ready?"

"It's already sitting at your table," she replied. She removed his tie from her neck and placed it over Logan's head.

"Look," Blanchard said, losing patience. "I need that seven fifty form."

22

Logan turned slowly around. It was no longer possible to ignore Blanchard, but it might be possible to get rid of him.

"Of course you do," he said. "What is it?"

"The seven fifty?" Blanchard was incredulous. "The monthly composite on trials and verdicts. Do you have it?"

"No. I turned in an eight twenty-two instead."

Blanchard looked lost. "There is no eight twenty-two."

"Well, there should be."

With that, Logan opened the Marchek file again and immersed himself in it. Unheeded, exasperated, Blanchard started to leave. Then he turned back with a final warning.

"I'll expect that form by the end of the day, Logan."

He received no response at all. Giving one last sigh of disgust, he walked out.

Freeman checked her boss' diary. "You've got lunch with the Chief today."

Logan was still studying the case. "Twelve thirty in his office . . ."

"One o'clock at Le Zinc."

"One o'clock at Le Zinc." Logan closed the file and began to rise. "The Marchek case—who's the defense?"

He was moving again; Freeman was right by his side. "Laura J. Kelly. She once tried to put a dog on the witness stand."

"Under oath?"

The two left the office, still talking, still walking. Doreen just shook her head, watching them go. She did not know how Logan did it; she was glad, however, to be there when he did.

The Marchek case may have been a bore, Logan thought, but at least it provided some entertainment: namely, defense attorney Laura Kelly.

Kelly was a petite, lively brunette who seemed as confident in her manner as she was skewed in her technique. She was willing to present the most—to use a polite word—unorthodox evidence and witnesses with the most unshakable conviction. This went a long way towards impressing the jury but not Logan. He had to admire her chutzpah, however, and her legs. He thought she might be fun to take on—in court, that is.

Right now, she was pleading the case of one Howard Marchek. He was a small, squat, sleazy fellow who sat at the defense desk wearing the benign smile of an angel. Behind him, about two dozen of his relatives sat like a silent cheering section. Kelly set forward her summation using searing eye contact and beautifully timed rhetoric.

Too bad, he thought, that I'm going to tear her to pieces.

"Mr. Marchek is a beloved member of a very large and close-knit family," she said. "We've brought forth more than two dozen of his cousins, aunts, uncles and in-laws. Each of them has testified under oath that the alleged stolen property was given to Mr. Marchek by them as birthday presents."

Logan smiled a little and shook his head. What a defense!

"Fourteen of these relatives," she went on, "chose to give him TV sets. An unlikely coincidence? Under normal circumstances, perhaps. But we have heard Mr. Marchek's own sworn testimony that all he wanted was a sort of 'media room,' not unlike that of the President of the United States."

Marchek spoke up, helpfully. "I got this passion for public affairs, Judge."

Judge Bailey banged his gavel. "Counsel will control her client."

"Sorry," Kelly said; then she turned to her client. "Mr. Marchek, your sense of outrage is understandable, but please . . ."

Logan watched in disbelief. This just keeps getting better and better, he thought. Yet to his amazement the jury was buying it. He knew a rapt jury when he saw one. Show me another trick, Kelly, he thought.

Kelly proceeded to. She turned back to the jury, taking on an expression of infinite gravity. "Now then. The prosecution has made a big issue out of the fact that none of his relatives could produce a receipt for the merchandise."

Suddenly, Kelly reached out and grabbed the wrist of a male juror. She looked at his hand and then up into his surprised eyes.

"That's a lovely watch, Sir," she said. "Do you have a receipt for it? No receipt? Clerk, arrest this man! Charge him with receiving stolen property."

Logan had to restrain a laugh. This one was too good not to spoil. He rose.

"I object, Your Honor," he said. "Defense counsel is fondling one of the jurors."

With a wave of her hand, Kelly took back the tactic. Yet she continued to address the man she had accosted, her certain eyes boring into his.

"The truth is," she said, "you're no thief, and neither is Howard Marchek. Receipts come—receipts go."

Logan looked up to the ceiling, as if for heavenly guidance. Kelly continued.

"So when one over-zealous detective approaches poor Mr. Marchek with an offer to buy one of his televisions for a hundred dollars . . ."

"Hey," Marchek interrupted, "I'm a man with fourteen TVs and a big heart . . ."

Judge Bailey rapped his gavel again, amidst a chorus of approval from Marchek's "relatives." Kelly threw a stern look at her client. Then, unfazed, she went on.

"Ladies and Gentlemen, my client is not a criminal—but a victim. A victim of circumstance, and his own special sense of generosity." She began to pace, dramatically. "Facing an organized pattern of entrapment, Howard Marchek reacted like any compassionate human being. Have we now, in this society, finally decided to reward kindness with a jail term? For all our sakes—I hope not."

She stopped then, suddenly, and turned. "Ladies and Gentlemen,

I ask each of you to look into your own heart, put yourself in Howard Marchek's place—and return a verdict of not guilty."

Kelly bowed her head, as if to say, I thank you so much for your time. Then she returned to the defense table. Logan gave her a little grin, but she looked forward, not acknowledging him. He rose.

With a completely contrasting casualness, he approached the jury. He flashed a nice warm smile.

"Before I make my final remarks," he began, "I'd like to congratulate Ms. Kelly on a defense which has been so entertaining and imaginative, I must confess I was torn between refuting it and simply giving her a round of applause."

He smiled again at Kelly, but she was having none of it. He turned back to the jury.

"I've chosen not to refute it, because we're not in a theater now—we're in a court of law, and in court we have to deal with the facts."

Logan wandered over to a table which had been piled high with items entered as exhibits: blenders, radios, TVs, hair dryers. Marchek's "gifts."

"We've all received our share of birthday presents. Last year, my daughter, Jennifer, gave me this very attractive tie . . ." He showed it and smiled. "Well . . . we like it. But all known generosity seems to pale when compared to the attention lavished on Howard Marchek by his adoring . . . relatives."

He gestured at the table. "It must have been quite a party. Detectives found TV sets, stereos, typewriters, microwaves—as detective-sergeant Anthony Santini observed the following morning, 'Maybe not the kind of variety you're gonna find at Sears & Roebuck, but definitely selling at much better prices.' "

Several jurors chuckled at this. Logan turned to Kelly once more. She still wouldn't look at him, but her gloomy face spoke volumes. Even she knows this one's mine, he thought.

Logan left the courtroom at his usual breathless pace and with an additional spring in his step. He liked a challenge, of course; but there was also something fun about winning hands-down immediately. Especially against someone as cracked as Laura Kelly.

"Mr. Logan! . . . Logan! . . . Slow down!"

Logan wasn't used to hearing Kelly's voice when it wasn't saying something inane. He stopped and turned, slowly.

Kelly reached him, out-of-breath. Her face showed no traces of remorse or rancor. She was as completely confident as she had been in the court, even upon hearing "Guilty."

"Twenty-seven relatives," Logan said. "Birthday presents. You were serious?"

"It was all I had," she answered. "It was the best possible defense."

"I'll give you points for originality, but the Marchek case should never have gone to court. You should have pleaded him guilty at the arraignment."

"Think of it this way," she said, "perhaps a new idea for you. Every person, guilty or innocent, deserves a defense. It's in the Constitution. You could look it up."

Logan made a sour face. He started walking again. She was hot on his tail.

"Why are you following me, Kelly?" Logan asked.

"I want to prevent a miscarriage of justice. I'd like you to talk to one of my clients, Chelsea Deardon."

Logan felt a pang when he heard that name: a feeling of what? Empathy? Desire? He did not know. But he was sure as hell not going to reveal himself to Kelly.

"I plan on talking to Chelsea Deardon," he said. "In court."

He turned a corner, thinking he might lose her. Unfortunately, no such luck.

"It's not the actual trial that concerns me," Kelly said. "There are some circumstances surrounding this case I'd like to brief you on informally."

"Well, if they're compelling enough . . ."

"They are."

"Then I'm sure a jury will agree with you." Logan gave her another grin. "Now, if you'll excuse me . . ."

He disappeared through the front door of the building, swiftly. Once outside, he took a deep breath, free of the Criminal Court's bad air and Kelly's bad ideas.

Then he realized he wasn't alone. Kelly's hand was on his arm.

"Look, I'm talking about evidence a jury may not get the chance to *hear*," she said, tugging on him, slowing him down. "You have a reputation for fairness. Someone who's more concerned with the truth than hanging another legal scalp on his wall."

Logan stopped. Was that what he was known for? He could not help it, he found himself listening to Kelly more seriously now. But not for long.

"Chelsea Deardon is very important to me," she said. "Someone I really believe in."

He sighed. "Like Howard Marchek?"

"That's it? That's the entire extent of your curiosity?"

"On the contrary. Twenty-seven relatives, a talking dog—I can hardly wait to see what you come up with this time."

Just then, Freeman drove a city-owned car up to the curb. Logan turned to Kelly. She was about to come back at him, but he didn't give her a chance.

"See you in court," he said.

She looked kind of cute, Logan thought, standing there like that. Silently.

Chapter Three

Logan was straightening his tie as Freeman pulled up in front of Le Zinc. He had been to the restaurant countless times—so had any lawyer—but never to meet Maxwell Bower, District Attorney of the State of New York.

He got out of the car and walked into the place. Immediately, he was cornered by a young attorney he knew only as Shaw.

"Tom, I need your legal opinion on something," he said.

"Call me later. I've got lunch with the Chief."

He walked farther into the restaurant's noisy, informal interior. Shaw followed.

"I'll make it quick. My client slams his truck through the window of a Seven-Eleven, right? Breaks a customer's leg, bangs up the clerk with bruises."

Logan was busy looking for Bower. "You've got a problem."

"Maybe not, hear me out. Okay, my client is driving, sure, that's a given. But he also has this girl with him who is resting her head on his lap—actively."

"Actively? Speak English."

"Resting her head—with affection. This naturally interfered with his concentration on driving. I think I can build a case on this. I mean, ultimately, the accident was *her* fault, not his. Got an opinion?"

"Yes. Sell the screen rights."

Logan passed Shaw and walked into Le Zinc's main dining room. In the corner, he spotted Bower, already seated. He was sixty-two, white-haired, enormously tall, and enormously intimidating.

Logan joined him at the table.

"You're late," Bower said, calmly. "That caused me stress. My doctor said I should cut down on stress."

"Sorry, Chief."

Bower dropped two small pills into a cup of steaming coffee. Logan watched him, apprehensively. He thought this was an awfully chummy place to meet. He wondered what Bower had in mind.

"These pills are supposed to kill the acid in the coffee before the acid in the coffee kills me," Bower explained. "I used to put a little brandy in to kill the acid. But I can't do that any more. No cigars, no brandy, no fatty meats. I'm going to have my doctor brought up on a charge of attempted murder."

Logan feigned a face of extreme interest to Bower. Get to the point, he thought.

"I want to get right to the point here," Bower said then. "I've always had the highest personal regard for you, Tom, both as a lawyer and a human being."

Logan flushed. "Well, thanks, I appreciate that."

"That's why I picked you to give the keynote at that banquet tonight. Every year some poor sonofabitch has to get up in front of that crowd and spout some comforting crap about how we're winning the war against crime. Well, this year, I wanted them to hear it from someone with style and charisma. This year, I wanted them to hear it from my choice for their next district attorney."

Logan thought he had not heard right. He stared at Bower, stunned. There was no mistaking it, that's what he had said. The old devil! Logan sat back slowly in his seat.

"This is my last year, Tom," Bower said. "I'm hanging it up. I'm going to go home, introduce myself to my wife and kids, find out if I have a dog and sit in front of a TV and watch the Mets break my heart."

Logan was hanging happily on every word. It was a second before he registered another voice cutting in.

"Phone call for you, Mr. Logan," a waiter was saying.

Logan looked up. He nodded an apology to Bower. Then he stood, slowly, still dazed by the turn of events.

Logan picked up the phone in a booth in Le Zinc's lobby. "Hello?"

A voice said, "Are you aware that the painting Chelsea Deardon tried to steal was painted by her father and in fact belonged to her?"

"Who the hell . . . Kelly?"

Logan looked through the booth's glass doors. In the restaurant lobby, he saw Laura Kelly, talking to him from another booth.

"Listen," she said, "about that painting . . ."

Logan didn't listen. He slammed the phone down furiously. Then he came out of the booth and found his waiter.

"No more calls," he told him. "For any reason."

The nerve of her, he thought. And right in the middle of the biggest news of my life. He made his way quickly back to Bower's table. He sat down again in his seat.

"Sorry, Chief."

"Well," Bower said, "what's the answer? Tom, you do well tonight and then if you want the job, I'll back you all the way. Interested?"

Logan paused, more for effect than anything else. Then he answered.

"Definitely interested."

Chapter Four

Kelly was not giving up without a fight. She stood in the telephone booth, trying it one more time.

"What do you mean, no more calls?" she said. "Mr. Logan asked me specifically to call him at this precise time."

There were no takers; there was not even a reply. All she got for her efforts was a dial tone. She proceeded to dial again. Then there was a soft tapping on the door.

She turned and saw a small bald man, his entire head red from the annoyance of waiting. Kelly yanked open the booth door.

"Lady," the man said, "if you don't hurry it up in there, I'm going to reach out and touch someone."

Kelly put on a face of righteous outrage. "Sir, I am an attorney. Are you aware that it's a felony in the state of New York to interrupt an attorney while she's making a phone call?"

If it hadn't been a law before, it was now: Laura Kelly had made it one. The man rushed away.

In her childhood, it had been kicking and screaming. Laura Kelly had used them whenever she wanted something bad enough. As an adult, she refined her tactics to include sound reasoning, persistence and a completely unflappable obstinace. It was a man's world and a cruel world, at that, but all was fair when you wanted something done. Especially if it was the right thing.

That was something Kelly never doubted: what was right and what was wrong. Unlike other people, she had no moments of self-doubt, no moments of embarrassment or hesitation. She always just barreled through. It left her without a husband and with many ex-boyfriends who had fled in exasperation. (She had never doubted that they were wrong in their reasoning and right to leave.) It also left her with an erratic career and the stunned disbelief of many of her colleagues. But she never doubted that she would be vindicated in the end.

That included the Chelsea Deardon case. If Tom Logan insisted on being pigheaded about it, then she would just have to take the initiative. He was a bright man and would see the light eventually. Kelly would just shine it so brightly in his eyes that he wouldn't be able to turn away.

So if Logan were at a banquet tonight and Kelly was not invited, she would just *be* invited, that's all. She put on her fanciest dress and gave Chelsea a call.

Kelly and Chelsea arrived at the Parker-Meridien Hotel after the affair had begun. The two women strode with utter confidence through the front door and past the luxurious lobby. They would have wafted right into the banquet itself if an usher hadn't stopped them.

"Your invitations, please," he said.

Kelly gave him a polite, brittle smile that meant, But of course. She handed him two pieces of paper and, with Chelsea in tow, went right on in. Kelly didn't even give him a chance to discover they were parking tickets.

Inside, the banquet room was packed with elegant, beautifully dressed members of New York's legal and political communities. Local TV crews followed the proceedings with mini-cams; reporters from papers cornered their prey and grilled them.

On the dais was a collection of V.I.P.s, including those in the top echelon of city government. Seated beside them was a happy but nervous Tom Logan, dressed in a slightly worn tux. He was listening carefully to the words of his superior and mentor Maxwell Bower, who stood pontificating at the podium.

" . . . but this is it, folks," Bower was saying. "This is finally it. This is my last year as your District Attorney."

A loud chorus of "No!" "Come on!" came from the otherwise dignified crowd. Bower raised his big hands in a good-natured call for silence.

"Too late," he said. "The appeal is denied. The verdict stands. Now then, the big question is . . . who will replace me?"

Bower paused, theatrically. There was a smattering of laughter and applause. Then he turned to Logan, whose smiling face said, Get on with it already.

"Well, perhaps, someone like our keynote speaker here tonight. For the past twelve years, I've given this man the toughest assignments and the heaviest case load. And for one simple reason—he gets the job done. Ladies and gentlemen, a man whose past performance guarantees him a brilliant future: Tom Logan!"

The crowd responded with a strong round of applause. Logan rose and accepted it with a small, self-effacing wave. The applause took awhile to subside. When it did, he grew serious. He cleared his throat and began.

"An attorney has to know the truth. Whether he attacks it or defends it, the truth is the indisputable touchstone of his trade.

And that's the tricky part, because his clients often lie to him, even when they're innocent." He flashed a nice smile to take the sting out of his words. "I don't know what it is about all of us, but it's human nature to lie to a lawyer."

The crowd chuckled. Not bad, Logan thought. A little gravity, a little charm, a little tease, a little truth. The audience seemed to be eating it up.

Suddenly, there were people in the audience whom he hadn't expected. Coming down the aisle, walking with frightening determination, was Laura Kelly. She was all dolled up, but her intentions were obviously less appealing than her appearance. Behind her, revealed only as Kelly passed, was Chelsea Deardon.

He had never seen her in the flesh. Freed from the prison of the TV screen, she was even more striking. She wore a diaphanous white gown, which showed her willowy figure to great advantage. Her blonde hair fell gracefully below her shoulders. And as always, there was her face, which displayed as much vulnerability as strength, as much hurt as sensuality.

To his amazement, his stares were returned. Chelsea's eyes locked with his. He could see her whisper to Kelly, "Is that him?"

All this did nothing at all to help his speech. He spoke now as if he were a million miles away.

"If your client was five miles from the scene of the crime, he'll probably tell you he was ten miles away. Nobody trusts a lawyer enough to tell him the truth . . ."

It was not just Chelsea's astonishing gaze that distracted him now. It was the fact that Kelly was approaching the dais itself. It was the fact that she was approaching Maxwell Bower.

Logan began to speak as if he were reading phonetically.

"Because of that—because we are what we are—that is to say, because we tend to . . ."

Kelly was whispering to Bower now. The audience began to whisper about her whispering. Bower actually rose and stepped away with the two women. Nearly half of the audience was more interested in this scene, which was slowly turning heated. Bower and Kelly were gesturing angrily at each other; Chelsea was just calmly, quizzically listening.

Logan, meanwhile, was suffering.

"Because people lie to lawyers so often, it's important to develop an understanding, a concept of truth that is truthful, or at least lacking in deception." A truthful truth? Somebody help me, he thought. "That way, we can get at the basic truth of things." Good going, Logan.

The argument off to the side was not cooling down; if anything, it was starting to flare even hotter. Now not only was the audience engrossed but the media was, too. Camera crews started slowly turning their lenses to the large, fuming D.A. and the small, obdurate Defense Attorney.

Logan quickly regained his train of thought in order to reach a coherent conclusion.

"A prosecuting attorney in particular must develop the instinct of a predator when it comes to determining the truth. Even when it turns out to be against his own best instincts. He must expose the truth. That's called justice. That's why I'm an attorney. Thank you."

The applause was a little bit more than polite. Logan acknowledged it, as he glanced over to catch the decision in the Kelly-Bowers brawl. He saw his boss nodding in what seemed agreement to Kelly's demands. Then Kelly turned and gave him an infuriating smile, wink and thumbs-up sign. As if they were on the same side!

Logan waved once more to the audience. Then he took his seat again, as Bower approached him.

"What was that all about?" Logan said.

"Kelly wants to file a complaint in the Deardon case. I told her no, and she threatened to call a press conference on the spot."

"So, what did you tell her?"

"I told her you'd examine the complaint. A quick investigation, it's over. We don't need this kind of press."

Logan felt furious—at Kelly for being so presumptuous and Bower for being so cowardly and political. He could not help himself, he shook his head no.

"I'm not going to do it," he said. "To hell with Kelly."

He glanced over. Kelly was watching them, carefully, seeking any clue to Logan's reaction. He gave her one: he mouthed the word "No" very distinctly.

Kelly shrugged back, as if to say, Suit Yourself. Then she turned to a reporter and gave him an encouraging nod. The man's camera turned on. He eagerly approached her with a microphone.

Logan could just barely make out what the reporter was saying, but what he could hear he didn't like.

"Moments ago," he began, "Laura J. Kelly, a Manhattan attorney, told us she planned to file charges against the District Attorney's office." He turned to Kelly. "Ms. Kelly, can you tell us what this is all about?"

Logan cursed to himself. This went beyond charming eccentricities and laughable theatrics; this was downright subversion. And on the night of the most important appearance of his career.

He rose, swiftly, and headed quickly down the dais towards Kelly. Before he could get there, however, a wall of reporters blocked his way, all trying to interview Kelly.

She, meanwhile, was more than happy to give her side of the story.

"I apologize for my conduct here tonight," she said, "but a public display of this kind is the only avenue left to us."

She directed a hand towards Chelsea, who stood there, looking naturally, beautiful and wounded. Cameras whirred in unison, taking all of her in.

"This young woman," Kelly went on, sonorously, "has been victimized by some very unscrupulous people. We've been trying to get cooperation from the D.A.'s office, but so far they've been stonewalling us. We have no choice but to file a complaint against the district attorney in this matter."

At last, Logan was able to burst through the media crush. He appeared, as if on cue, much to the reporters' delight.

He looked with abject disbelief at Kelly.

"I see we have Tom Logan of the District Attorney's office here," the reporter said.

All microphones and cameras now left Chelsea and landed on Logan. He grew a little pale under such scrutiny; Kelly had actually seemed to brighten and grow rosier on camera. He cleared his throat.

"Mr. Logan," the reporter went on, "what can you tell us about this situation?"

"Well . . ." Logan had to raise his voice to be heard, "naturally, all of this comes as a total surprise to me. But I'm certain that any implication of impropriety on the part of our office is totally unfounded. I'll take personal charge of this case from now on, and I assure you that justice will be served."

The microphones swung at once back to Kelly; the cameras soon followed. She looked at Logan with patronizing admiration, impressed by his grace and class under such pressure.

"I'd like to say that I expected nothing else from a man of Tom Logan's character and reputation. I was sure that once he'd been made aware of my client's predicament, he would take quick and decisive action."

Kelly directed a twinkling smile at Logan now. Flashbulbs popped, recording the dramatic happy ending.

Logan only shook his head. This time she's won, he thought. I am really in this thing now.

Chapter Five

The bar in Soho was not the kind of place in which to wear a tuxedo. It was also not the kind of place Logan would ever go to. New Wave artists, punk rockers, transvestites, hangers-on: all the denizens of the nineteen eighties downtown scene packed the place nightly.

Tonight, it played host to an Assistant District Attorney, a defense attorney and her client. All in formal wear. It had been, needless to add, Kelly's idea.

She had taken no time to crow about her coup in snagging Logan's attention and cooperation. That was not her style. She moved right into the next order of business, as if patting herself on the back would be digressive. She had, after all, been right from the start.

Logan was feeling a little buzzed, not only from the peculiar atmosphere, but from the evening in general. He had gone from being publicly endorsed for D.A. to being publicly challenged to a duel. To top it all off, he was now sitting knee-to-knee with Chelsea Deardon, not the best position to be in when he had to work to send her to jail.

She looked at him with a nearly hypnotic stare. He had to return a neutral, businesslike look. He secretly felt she was staring right through his clothes to his skin—and right through his skin to his soul.

Sitting beside them, Kelly just smiled, like a genial and dogged host finally successful in arranging a blind date.

"Well," she beamed, "it took a bit of gentle persuasion, but we're finally all together. Mr. Logan—I'm sure you have a few questions . . ."

Logan made a face at Kelly. Give me a break, he thought. Then he turned to Chelsea, who remained silent, as if indeed entranced. Like a sexy zombie, Logan thought.

"For the record," he began, "so there are no misunderstandings, you have the right to remain silent . . ."

Kelly interrupted, nodding. "Anything you say may be used against you."

"If you're not entirely thrilled with your attorney, one will be provided for you."

Kelly looked away, tolerantly. Chelsea managed a smile, which gave her face a new element: warmth. Logan had to ignore that, too.

"Oh, no," Chelsea said. "I like her."

She had a nice voice, he decided, but bad taste. Kelly turned back, with a smile of vindication.

Logan decided to cut through the chit-chat. He changed his look from neutral to confrontational.

"Did you steal that painting?" he asked Chelsea.

"Well, yes," Kelly answered for her.

"Yes but no," Chelsea clarified.

This, of course, did not clarify things at all.

"Which is it?" Logan said, bluntly.

"Both," Kelly replied.

Logan sighed and made to leave. "This is a waste of my time."

40

His tactic shook Chelsea, as he had hoped it would. She put up a hand to keep him there.

"I did try to steal the painting, but it already belonged to me."

There was a pause. All right, Logan thought, that's a start. He returned to his seat. Chelsea's eyes lost part of their mesmeric quality; they became filled instead with embarrassment. Finally, she lowered her gaze to the table.

"Can you prove that?" Logan asked.

"My father gave me that painting when I was eight years old," she said. "He even dedicated it to me in writing on the back. All anybody has to do is look."

Chelsea closed her eyes. She saw it all then: the party, the people, the presents, and the fire. She wished at once to stay in the memory and to escape it. Her eyes slowly reopened.

Logan was staring right at her, obviously eager to pursue the hitherto unmentioned inscription on the painting. But he was interrupted by the appearance of a young companion of Kelly's.

He was wearing sunglasses, though the place was dark. He wore loose, fashionably ill-fitting pants and a Keith Haring T-shirt. He was in his early twenties.

"Laura, is that *you?*" he asked. He checked out her dress. "*Very* attractive . . ." Then he checked out Logan. "Is she your lawyer, too?"

Before Logan could answer—not that he was about to—the young artiste had moved on to another table and another close friend.

"Conrad Box," Kelly said. "Sculptor. Fairly well known. I helped him fight an eviction. He paid me with a blender. I mean, a painting of a blender. He does appliance art."

"I hate neo-realists," Chelsea said to Logan, "don't you?"

Logan had no opinion; he was thrown off his train of thought. Then shaking his head as if to clear it, he continued.

"Do you have any other proof that the painting once belonged to you?"

41

"My father kept a journal," Chelsea answered.

"Like a diary?"

"Sketches, ideas, all kinds of things."

Kelly turned, put out. "You didn't tell me that."

Chelsea was oblivious of her. "There are sketches of that painting in his journal and beside one of them, he wrote: 'For Chelsea's eighth birthday.' "

"I'd like to see that journal," Logan said.

"It's in my apartment," Chelsea said, suggestively. "You can come by any time."

It was not the answer Logan had expected, or wanted. He could not keep a small chill from crossing his shoulders, however.

"Thanks for the invitation," Kelly said, mistakenly. "I'll be there."

Then Logan felt a bigger chill. Under the table, Chelsea's long leg had found his own. It was not just a casual, accidental brushing; she was slowly pressing her calf against his calf, her thigh against his. All the while her eyes showed no trace of her actions, not a hint of desire.

Logan felt ambivalent about this occurrence. Naturally, he greatly enjoyed it; he also felt it might have an unnatural effect on his case. With a good deal of reluctance, trying to seem nonchalant, he slowly moved his leg away from hers.

This little mating dance had not escaped the notice of Kelly. She directed an unkind stare at both her client and her legal adversary.

"Who owns the painting?" Logan asked Chelsea.

"Robert Forrester," Kelly cut in. "Major developer."

"What were you doing at his place?" he asked Chelsea, pointedly.

"His wife throws parties for young artists," she said. "That way, people think she knows art. She's bored. She likes to wear earrings."

"What's the painting worth?"

"Two hundred thousand," Kelly answered, "ballpark figure."

Logan was surprised. "Your father must have made a lot of money."

"I guess," Chelsea said, indifferently.

"What kind of an inheritance did you receive?"

"None."

Kelly explained. "The estate was bankrupt."

Logan thought a minute. He trusted Chelsea; any defendant who was so brazenly flirtatious with her prosecutor had to be either innocent or stupid. He did not think she was stupid.

"All right," he said. "Tomorrow, we'll go look at the painting. If there's an inscription on the back, I'll consider dropping the charges."

This cheered Chelsea; she smiled with the gaiety of a child. Kelly, on the other hand, still looked suspiciously at the two of them. She did not know if she were thrilled about this turn of events.

Chapter Six

If the bar in Soho had been too downtown for Logan, the apartment of Robert Forrester the next day was far too high-class.

He couldn't believe how this guy lived: in a duplex penthouse, decorated in stark gray and white, with as few furnishings as were absolutely necessary. It boasted a giant picture window, which afforded anyone a magnificent view of Central Park. It was the ultimate in cold elegance. So was its owner.

He was fifty-five, but he was remarkably well-preserved. His skin was taut and tanned, his hair cut impeccably short. He wore a chic white sweater over white pants. This matched ideally the stunning black ebony table at which he sat, pouring coffee. The table sat twelve but today it only sat Forrester, Logan and Kelly.

Chelsea, of course, was not there but her presence still haunted the place—for all three of them. Logan still felt her leg against his; Kelly still felt resentful; Forrester looked as if he had trouble feeling anything.

"I'm afraid I can't show the Deardon to you, Mr. Logan," he was saying. "I don't own it any longer."

Logan paused. "I don't understand."

"I traded it this morning."

Kelly butted in. "Traded it? To whom?"

Forrester looked over at her, slightly peevishly. He spoke as if to a child. "To a gallery."

"Which gallery?" Logan asked.

"Taft Gallery."

Just then, a Spanish maid entered. She set a steaming plate of eggs before them, and went back into the kitchen.

The interruption annoyed Kelly as much as the information. "Mr. Forrester, that painting is material evidence in a felony proceeding."

"Not any more," Forrester said. "You see, I've decided to drop all charges against Chelsea."

There was a long pause. Logan looked at Kelly; Kelly looked at Logan. Then they both looked back at the implacable Forrester, who had, after all, brought the charges of robbery in the first place.

"What?" Kelly said.

"Why?" Logan asked.

"Her father and I were good friends," Forrester replied. "Chelsea's had a rather . . . difficult childhood. It's obvious to me she acted on impulse. There was no harm done."

"If you don't mind my curiosity, Mr. Forrester," Logan said, "exactly what did you get in return for the Deardon?"

Forrester did not reply. He only turned to his right, looked to a certain place and smiled.

On the wall was a painting of a woman's face in which there seemed to be two faces intertwined, visible from every side. It was boldly colored, primitive in rendering, yet enormously sophisticated in meaning.

Logan did not reply. He just thought it was kind of a weird painting. But Kelly sat up straight in her chair.

"A Picasso for a Deardon?" she asked, aghast.

Forrester gave a thin, sly smile.

"Yes. I thought it was a rather good trade, as well."

From the Forrester apartment, Logan and Kelly proceeded downtown to Fifty-seventh Street, home of many of Manhattan's top galleries. The Taft was between Fifth and Madison Avenues.

Logan had yet to register any problems in what Forrester had told them. All the way downtown, however, Kelly walked in troubled silence.

They reached the gallery just in time to see a huge Rauschenberg painting being lifted inside. Like a piano, it was being carried by a large crane into the gallery's window, which was on the second floor. Traffic was backed up for blocks because of it; drivers honked and called out obscenities. The painting may have been abstract but the problem was concrete, the reaction basic.

Before they entered, Logan felt obliged to inquire into Kelly's funk, for he felt he might have missed something. He proceeded gingerly, not wishing to display his artistic ignorance.

"So Taft traded a Picasso for a Deardon . . ." he began, idly.

Kelly did not reply. He had no choice but to be crass.

"That's not a good trade?"

She shook her head. "Not for a gallery owner who intends to stay in business very long."

She looked at him then with familiar condescension, as if she knew what would be for the best. "No offense, but since I know something about art, you'd better let me do the talking inside the gallery."

"Look," Logan said, irritably, "let's just understand something right now. I don't know much about art. I know a great deal about a lot of other things, but I've never learned . . . no, actually, I've never *cared* much about art."

That should fix her, he thought. But Kelly heard the defensive tone in his voice and she happened to notice the blush in his cheeks.

"It's all right," she said, kindly. "You don't have to feel insecure about it."

Logan opened his mouth to offer more offended protests, but Kelly was way ahead of him, through the gallery's front door.

Why don't you try me on Gene Kelly movies, he thought, then we'll see who knows what.

The Taft contained some of the most acclaimed—and expensive—modern art in the city. Henry Moore sat under Anthony Caro; Robert Longo hung next to Chuck Close.

Logan and Kelly approached the front desk, where a young male receptionist was stationed.

Logan did the honors. "Mr. Logan and Ms. Kelly to see Victor Taft. He's expecting us."

"If you'll wait here a minute . . ." the assistant said, and went to check.

Kelly wandered into the gallery's main room. She looked about, appreciatively, mumbling the identifications of paintings to herself. Then she raised her voice a bit, to make sure Logan could hear her.

"A De Kooning . . ." she noted, "A Miro . . . A Calder over there . . ."

Logan only grinned. "How about that . . ."

Then there was a third voice breaking into the gallery's quiet. It had an air of class and culture Logan's and Kelly's could not match.

"Mr. Logan?"

Logan turned around. Victor Taft entered the room. He was in his late forties but, like Robert Forrester, seemed if not younger then ageless. He was not effeminate but there was something sensual and a bit cruel about him.

In his elegant clothes, he seemed an unpredictable, volatile man who had been packaged in an appealing, presentable manner. He looked like the offspring of Business and Art.

"I'm Victor Taft," he said. "Thank you for calling in advance. I have a very busy schedule, as I'm sure you will appreciate."

"We'll try to be brief," Logan said. "This is Laura Kelly."

"A pleasure."

"What a magnificent gallery," Kelly said, knowledgeably.

Taft seemed impatient with her show of erudition. "How nice of you to notice. Now then . . ."

Logan followed his lead and got down to business. "Mr. Taft, do you happen to have any Picassos here at the present time?"

"Why, yes. As a matter of fact," Taft said, "you're standing right in front of one."

Logan turned, very, very slowly. He saw a sparely drawn, black-and-white lithograph of Don Quixote and Sancho Panza. He turned back.

"Oh, of course." He smiled, uneasily. "Uh, expensive?"

"Value is a relative thing," Taft replied. "Picasso is one of the true masters of this century."

Kelly cut in. "And yet you traded a Picasso for a Deardon that couldn't possibly have been worth as much."

"That particular Deardon," Taft countered, calmly, "was one of his last paintings, a work of total confidence and maturity. Deardon was my discovery and so I feel rather proprietary about his work. I've pestered Robert Forrester to part with it for years, so I was thrilled when he finally agreed."

Logan turned to Kelly, humbled enough to seek some expert advice. She made a private, skeptical face.

"We'd like to see the Deardon," Logan said to Taft, "if you don't mind."

"Certainly," he answered, unruffled. "It's sitting in my office. I don't believe it's even been uncrated yet."

Taft's office was nicer than Logan's apartment. It had been carefully and tastefully decorated and sported several famous Calders, Miros and Giacomettis. Logan and Kelly and Taft waited while the receptionist, Roger, carefully uncrated a painting lying on top of a work table.

Logan's attention passed from Roger to a piece of art which

dominated the room. It was a seven foot tall sculpture, tall, tubular, imposing and very abstract. Kelly was already studying it, admiringly.

"That's a Bertolini," Taft said, noticing their stares. "Startling, isn't it? It was his model for a larger version which stands in Sutton Square Park."

Logan examined it, running his fingers over its smooth surface. "I suppose the price is equally startling . . ."

"It's not for sale. It was given to me personally by the artist. It has great sentimental value."

"If you don't mind my asking," Logan said, "what exactly was . . . or is . . . your relationship with Chelsea Deardon?"

This made the older man pause. He recovered quickly, however, without a trace of discomfort.

"Her father and I were very close. I watched Chelsea grow up." Taft's voice grew cold. "Mr. Logan. You're leaning."

Logan jumped; he had absent-mindedly rested an arm on a section of the Bertolini. He changed his position, smiling. He couldn't help it; it was comfortable.

"Sorry."

"Recently, Chelsea and I have lost touch," Taft went on, "although I've followed her career. Her sensibility of art doesn't interest me. She's a performance artist, you know . . . happenings . . . very ephemeral happenings . . ."

"She's a what?" Logan said.

It was Kelly who answered. "A performance artist."

"I hear she's quite talented," Taft said, archly. "Ah, thank you, Roger . . ."

The young assistant had finished removing the painting from its crate. Logan, Kelly and Forrester crossed to the work table to take a look.

The crate clearly had Robert Forrester's return address stamped on it. Kelly studied the painting with a critical eye.

"It's . . ." she chose her words carefully, "very powerful."

Logan was a bit more interested in the legal than in the artistic end. "I'd like to look at the back of the painting, if you don't mind."

"How refreshing," Taft said, with a straight face. "Most of my clients prefer to look at the front."

Kelly made a face at Logan, to say it served him right. Logan made an annoyed face back at her. Then Taft flipped the painting over.

It was blank; the canvas showed no sign of Deardon's signature. Now Kelly looked at him with a different expression: suspicion.

On their way back down Fifty-seventh Street, neither Logan nor Kelly said much at first. Yet each appeared opposite from the other: Logan was relaxed, convinced his work was done; Kelly was agitated, convinced her work was just beginning.

Finally, she turned and broke the silence.

"Talk about a stonewalling witness," she said. "That was the shiftiest performance I've seen in some time."

Logan shrugged. "I thought he was being pretty straight forward with us."

"You thought . . . ? Logan, what happened to that sixth sense you're supposed to be famous for? Doesn't all this feel just a little too neatly tied up for you?"

Logan stopped her. "Kelly—charges dropped, no signature. It's dead. Done."

Kelly stared defiantly at him, her mental wheels still racing. She began to further state her case when Logan politely cut her off.

"Come on," he said, "I'll get you a cab."

"I can get my own cab," she said, huffily, "thank you."

Kelly stepped out into the street directly in the path of an on-rushing cab. It screeched to a halt barely a foot in front of her. Unfazed, Kelly got in and took off.

Logan just shook his head and kept walking. He was glad for the time being at least that Kelly was out of his hair. Art expert, human nature expert, legal expert. It must be hard, he thought with a smile, to be such a genius about everything. Thank God *he* didn't have that problem.

There was one more thing to add to all the things that Logan did not know. There was a heavyset man watching him from across the street. This man aspired to be expert at only one subject: the whereabouts of Tom Logan and Laura J. Kelly.

Chapter Seven

That night, Logan couldn't sleep again.

He tried everything. He tried the side position: arms stretched out, one leg slightly bent. No dice. He switched to a Christ-like position: flat on his back, his arms spread. This position was never famous for being comfortable. He switched to the ever-popular fetal position: knees to chest, pillows gathered in tightly. This provided none of the comfort it was always rumored to provide. Finally, his eyes shot open and he tried another position: sitting up.

Logan did not know what exactly was troubling him. That is, he did not know which of his many troubles was the one keeping him awake. Bower's recommendation of him for District Attorney made him happy but anxious. Would he really get the job? Would he be able to do it after all his years of preparing for it? The prospect of losing Jennifer to the warm wasteland of Los Angeles made him simply anxious. Would Barbara find some way to take her that was legally foolproof—even for a professional like himself? Finally, Kelly's disquietude about the Deardon case made him annoyed. Why wasn't she satisfied about charges being dropped when *he* was the prosecutor and *he* was satisfied? His head suddenly felt as stuffed with problems as his apartment was with belongings.

There was one final consideration: Chelsea Deardon herself. Had she been lying or just confused about the painting? And why couldn't he face the idea of possibly never feeling her leg against his again?

Logan considered giving sleep another shot. Then he addressed a sigh towards the forces of worry which had defeated him:

"You win. Unconditional surrender . . ."

He made his way from the bedroom to the living room. There he approached his only roommate: a small Sony color TV. He turned it on and dialed through the stations.

At that hour, there were mostly religious shows and static on. But at his next stop, he found exactly what he was looking for.

It couldn't be more perfect: Gene Kelly. And not just Gene Kelly but Gene Kelly in his best and Logan's favorite movie, "Singin' in the Rain." And not just "Singin' in the Rain" but the best scene in "Singin' in the Rain": Gene's dance to the title song.

Logan sat close to the set, not wanting to miss a minute. Gene was just starting to dance his happy dance after falling in love with Debbie Reynolds. He was a man completely free for the moment of troubles, giving himself up to the most graceful physical expression of happiness.

Logan looked down. He noticed his own bare foot tapping slightly. He couldn't help himself, he had to join Gene.

With a softshoe—in this case, soft foot—step, he danced his way across the living room to the foyer. There he removed his own umbrella from a stand near the front door.

Twirling the thing, humming to himself, he tapped his way back to the TV set. There he danced along with Gene, aping his every step, twirling his umbrella identically. This could be a big new team, he thought. Astaire and Rogers. Logan and Kelly.

Actually, he didn't like the sound of *that* too much.

53

But it didn't matter. Here he was, tapping his troubles away, becoming a man separate from the cares of modern-day crime and modern-day divorce, living the glamor of a nineteen fifties MGM movie. Nothing could intrude on that.

Then the doorbell rang. and Logan's umbrella went twirling into a lamp.

It didn't just twirl into it. It slammed into it, sent the lamp crashing to the floor, breaking its bulb. For a grand finale, the umbrella popped open, as if curtseying.

Logan sighed. The doorbell rang again. Maybe it was a neighbor, complaining about the noise at such an early hour. What could they say to him, he wondered: "Hey, turn that happiness off"?

His carefree tap step became a depressed, leaden-footed shamble as he moved slowly to the front door. Behind it, he found no neighbor and not even a friend. He found someone who was something more than a stranger, but exactly what he did not yet know.

Chelsea Deardon.

She looked pale and afraid. Her lips quivered and her eyes darted back and forth, anxiously. She looked beautiful.

"Someone's following me," Chelsea said.

"*What?*"

"I'm scared."

"Where did you . . ."

"Can I come in?"

"Well . . . I guess . . . sure."

Logan slowly moved aside for her to enter. Then he shut the door behind her. Chelsea wrapped her arms around herself, nervously. She threw back her head so that her long hair cleared her face.

"Listen," Logan said, "how did you know where I lived?"

Chelsea was oblivious. Her voice shook. "I was afraid he'd follow me home."

"Who? Who'd follow you home?"

"The man."

"What man?"

"I don't know." She swallowed, calming herself. "But I've seen him three different times in three different places today."

"Where is he now, do you know?"

"Probably right out in front."

The answer sent a slight shiver down Logan's back. He saw the intensity in Chelsea's eyes, the apparent sincerity in her face. Then he moved slowly over to the window and looked out.

The street was empty.

"Well, I'm sorry, but I don't see anything."

"He's hiding." Chelsea was certain of it.

Logan sighed. He noticed that the young woman was making her way farther into his apartment. She took in everything he had with her hypnotic gaze.

"Chelsea," he said, "you can't stay here. Maybe at a friend's . . ."

She turned slowly around. Her eyes looked deeply into his. She spoke plaintively, pitiably. She did not speak above a whisper.

"I don't have a friend," she said.

They stood there like that, just looking at each other, for a long minute. Logan could not turn away from her, physically or emotionally. He could not imagine turning her out, or turning her out alone. Something about her made him need to protect her.

"I'll take you home," he said. "Hang on while I get dressed."

While Logan was changing from his pajamas into his clothes, Chelsea expanded her examination of his apartment. She peeked into boxes, checked out the books on his shelves, rifled through his record albums. She ran her fingers over his things, holding them for a minute, or simply trailing her fingertips along them. She searched his place with the inquisitiveness of a child and the sensuous touch of a woman.

Logan's voice from the bedroom made her jump.

"Did you talk to Kelly?" he asked.

"Earlier," she responded.

"Then you know that painting didn't have any writing on the back."

"And of course, you're sure Victor Taft showed you the right painting. You're both familiar enough with my father's work to tell one from another."

Logan reappeared then, buttoning the last button on his shirt. Chelsea's harder tone brought new confusion to his face, even a little trepidation.

What she had *said* struck him, as well. Suddenly, he did not trust the situation any more than Kelly did. He checked out the window again, just to be sure. But the street was still deserted.

"Let's go," he said.

Chapter Eight

Chelsea lived in the Soho area, in a converted warehouse. The place sat on a dark, shadowy side street across from several deserted and abandoned buildings. As they got out of their cab, Logan couldn't help checking behind and around himself.

He did so all the way to the front door of her building. He didn't stop once they got inside. The building was no brighter than the street; the stairway was dimly lit, filled with arching shadows and mysterious creaks and groans.

It was also filled with mysterious people, as Logan learned when they reached the second floor. An intense-looking man came out of his apartment on the first floor below them. Logan looked down at him. The man stopped and looked back, with dark, penetrating eyes. The man looked offended and no stranger to violence. Logan only gave him a silly, half-smile. The man sneered in return and went into the apartment across the hall. He slammed the door behind him.

When they reached the third floor landing, Chelsea took out her key and unlocked the second door down. Logan waited as she swung the door open. He would have just as soon bid her goodnight right there.

"Well . . ." he began.

"Come in," she said, matter-of-factly.

Reluctantly, glancing behind himself again, Logan did.

The apartment was very bare. The only furniture was a mattress lying in one corner. The walls were very tall and had once been white; the hardwood floor was dingy and scratched. The windows were very big and very dirty. A small kitchen area rounded it all off.

"Lots of space," was all Logan could think to say.

He saw something else then: near the windows, a mechanical apparatus had been placed. It contained speakers, amplifiers and other elements which he could not identify. It seemed carefully arranged, like part of a set in a stage play.

"What's that?" Logan said.

"What I do," Chelsea answered.

Logan was about to ask for clarification when he remembered: Chelsea was—what had Taft called it?—a performance artist. He smiled, politely. He still had no idea what it meant.

"Sit down," Chelsea said. "I'll show you."

Suddenly, the lights in the loft were switched off. At the same time, Chelsea flipped several switches on the apparatus near the window.

Seemingly out of nowhere, three life-sized photographs of Chelsea were illuminated. Each was a full-length view of her from a different angle; each brought out her disconcerting sensuality. In the bottom right-hand corner of each was a childlike drawing. The first was of a birthday cake, the second of a house; the third was of an artist's palette.

Pulsating music began to play. Carrying a small torch which she had lighted, Chelsea crossed to a three-dimensional replica of a birthday cake sitting in front of the cake picture. Chelsea set the cake aflame. It immediately exploded with a flash and was reduced to a smoldering wire frame.

Logan reeled backwards, the explosion shocking him. Chelsea was moving gracefully, rhythmically, in a quasi-dance, to replicas of the house and the palette. She lighted and exploded both in turn. Logan felt his shock decrease and his fascination grow.

Now she glided to one of the photographs of herself. She copied exactly the sleek, sensual pose of the photo. Then holding the lighted torch, she drifted behind it. Within a second, flames curled up from the picture's base, eating up and away at it. The fire soon consumed the picture whole.

All the while, Chelsea's voice was heard coming from a sound system. She was huskily whispering, "Put out the fire . . . Put out the fire . . ."

The picture was gone but Chelsea was not behind it. All that remained there was a three-dimensional replica of her. The music intensified; her recorded voice pleaded more urgently.

"Put out the fire . . . Put out the fire . . ."

Then Chelsea's replica, too, exploded, leaving only a smoking frame.

Logan found his fascination trading places with discomfort now. Smoke was filling the apartment; Chelsea was nowhere to be found. He reeled around and saw a fire extinguisher sitting in the corner. Printed on it in large, clear letters, beckoning in an Alice in Wonderland way, were the words, "PUT OUT THE FIRE."

Logan picked up the extinguisher with the intention of doing exactly that. He aimed the instrument, fired—and found that only more smoke came out. He heard a rumble of thunder claps; then a driving rain began.

Then everything instantly stopped.

There was total silence. Before him, the fire-blackened white bodycast of Chelsea—for this is what it had been—smoldered. There was not even a remnant of the smoke or flames. Logan looked around, mystified.

Then a hand touched him on the shoulder. He turned his head, startled. Chelsea stood next to him with a serene, slightly curious expression.

"Well," she said, calmly, "what did you think?"

Logan tried to calm his breathing before he could respond. His first instinct was to holler at her for unnerving him. Then he decided only to cross his arms and nod his head like the most detached critic.

"Well," he said, thoughtfully, "fine."

Her eyes burned into his. "What did you *think?*"

"I don't know," Logan said, honestly. "I felt . . . uncomfortable."

"Good," Chelsea said, with a smile. "That's what I'm trying to do, challenge your perspective, your way of seeing things. Make you uncomfortable."

Logan nodded; it made a sort of sense; it had certainly been effective. But before he could express any of these thoughts, Chelsea did something which took his mind off art.

She kissed him.

It was a long, lingering kiss, performed with just the right combination of warmth and desire. Logan let her kiss him and let her continue to kiss him. He did not, however, kiss her back. This at worst, he felt, made him only an accessory to the crime.

Chelsea withdrew her lips from his, slowly. She never withdrew her eyes.

"Still uncomfortable?" she whispered.

Logan was caught helplessly in her gaze. Then he managed to answer, "You bet."

He turned away, suddenly, a quick change being his only chance of resisting her. Then he resumed a business-like demeanor. "You said your father kept a journal. May I see it?"

Chelsea wasn't prepared for this sudden shift or for this question. She replied, falteringly, "I'd . . . have to find it first."

Logan glanced around the stark apartment. "Shouldn't take long."

"Maybe it's . . . down in the storeroom. I forget." She sounded like a drunk trying desperately to appear sober.

"When was the last time you saw it?"

"I . . . last week. Maybe longer. I can't remember."

Logan became the prosecutor now. "There is no journal, is there?"

"He kept a journal," she said, insistently.

"But you don't have it?"

"Do you always cross-examine people?"

"Only when they lie to me."

The apartment held a heady mix of passion and prosecution; it was making Chelsea dizzy. She spoke now as if giving herself completely up to hm, as if verbally fainting into his arms.

"I don't have anything from when my father was alive. There was a journal, there were paintings—and then there was a fire."

She turned away, hiding her eyes from the blaze in her mind. "I lied to you because I wanted you to trust me, to believe in me. I didn't think the truth was good enough."

She was drifting while speaking; she had drifted to the window. Now she stopped there and looked down.

"He's down there," she said.

"There's no one down there," Logan answered.

"I can feel it."

She looked at Logan as if she were positive. Logan only gave a long, weary sigh.

"Look," he said, "I've got to get some sleep."

"You can sleep here," she told him, simply.

61

Logan did not even answer. This was all too complicated; he wanted to be back fidgeting and fuming in his own lonely bed. He headed for the door.

"If there's any . . . *real* trouble, call the police. Nine-one-one. Emergency."

Chelsea nodded now, resigned to being resisted. She gave a brief, purely friendly smile.

"Thanks for taking me home," she said.

Logan returned the same smile. "Thanks for the . . . demonstration."

They each looked away at the same time then. Logan left the apartment and trotted down the stairs without looking back.

When he got to the front door, he suddenly hesitated. Chelsea's nervousness was getting to him. He opened the door silently and only partially.

Outside, a short distance down the street, a man's shadow could be seen, reflected by a street lamp.

Logan closed the door, carefully. Then he turned and found his way through the dim lobby to the building's back exit.

He tiptoed out into a rear garden. Stepping over plants and flowers in the dark, he walked like a blind man, hands waving before him, until he found a fence. He got a foothold on it. Then he climbed up until he reached the top. He looked down into a narrow alleyway.

"I can't believe I'm doing this," he mumbled.

Then he vaulted and dropped down. He slammed his foot into a trashcan and interrupted two trysting cats before he found his way from the alley out into the street.

He peered out onto the avenue. He looked one way and then the other. Everything seemed clear.

Then he saw him.

The man stood down the street, his back to Logan, staring up in the direction of Chelsea's apartment. He was heavyset and dressed entirely in black.

"Something interesting up there?" Logan asked.

The man wheeled around. His face was caught in the rays of a street lamp. Not a pretty face; a cruel face. The light also revealed a small pump shotgun held in his hands.

The man fired. Logan dived back into the alley, as the bullet ricocheted off a wall near his head. He kept his back pressed up fast against the alley wall as he heard the man dart away up the avenue.

After his steps faded in the distance, Logan peeled himself off the wall. He left the alley, stealthily. He crept to a telephone booth in the opposite direction from where the man had fled.

His heart thumping in his ears, Logan pushed a quarter into the phone. Then he quickly pumped Information, four-one-one.

"In Manhattan," he whispered, "the number of a Laura J. Kelly."

He did not know why he was calling her. Suddenly, she seemed like his best friend.

But all he got was a recording.

"Hi, this is Laura Kelly. I'm not able to come to the phone . . ."

Logan slammed the phone down. He waited a second. Then one more time, he dialed Information.

"Get me the police," he said.

Chapter Nine

That night, Kelly couldn't sleep, either.

The details of the Deardon case had gotten to her: what had Taft been up to? And had Chelsea really been leveling with her? She had had no choice but to do what she always did at a time like this: cook.

She didn't just cook eggs or whip up a salad. She threw together an entire Crab Louis. She chopped the onions, cut up the parsley, threw in the crab, and cooked the whole mess at just the right temperature.

While it was cooking, she had switched on a small TV she kept in the kitchen. The only thing on was the umpteenth rerun of "Singin' in the Rain," never one of her favorites. Musicals were entirely too frivolous for Kelly.

Just as Gene Kelly started to sing in the rain, she heard the oven timer ding. Pushing her hand into a pot holder, she opened up the stove.

"Awright, Louis," she imitated Bogart, "drop the gun. I'm comin' in . . ."

As usual, the dish was cooked exactly right; what did Kelly ever do that wasn't? As usual, she ate it all by herself sitting in her kitchen before the TV. And as usual, she fell asleep afterwards, right on the kitchen table.

She slept soundly enough so that she didn't hear the phone ring. She thought she heard something but it did not register enough to awaken her. She also thought she heard her phone machine pick up ("Hi, this is Laura Kelly. I'm not able to come to the phone . . .") but finally decided she was just dreaming.

What finally roused her was the doorbell.

It didn't ring just once. It rang and kept ringing, as if whoever had arrived would not be satisfied until someone, anyone, came to the door.

Kelly reached her hand out, groggily, for the telephone. When she found that it wasn't ringing, she directed her attention to the door. The sun was shining in her eyes. The TV no longer displayed Gene Kelly but Bryant Gumbel and Jane Pauley.

She stumbled the few steps to the door. The ringing had stopped. Now someone was knocking. She paused, warily.

"Who is it?" she said.

"Laura Kelly?" a man asked. "I want to talk to you."

Kelly didn't like the sound of him. "Get in touch with me at my office, all right?"

"Cavanaugh's the name. Detective C. J. Cavanaugh, Manhattan South."

Kelly thought a minute. Then, tightening the cord on her bathrobe, she opened the door, keeping the chain on.

"Let's see some I.D.," she said.

A man's hand holding a detective's shield was thrust through the narrow opening. The identification fit. Kelly undid the chain and opened the door.

A big, burly, blondish man entered. He gave a friendly smile to Kelly. He was carrying a thick folder under his arm.

"Sorry to bother you, Miss Kelly," he said. "It's about the Deardon case."

Kelly did not hesitate then. "Come in."

He lumbered in, giving a tiny nod of thanks. As soon as he came near the kitchen, he started sniffing the air, approvingly.

"What's for breakfast?" he asked.

"Angel's food cake, pumpkin pie and chocolate chocolate chip cookies," Kelly replied.

"Real ambitious to start the day. White sugar, processed flour, high cholesterol . . ."

"I take a vitamin supplement," Kelly said, quickly. "What about the Deardon case?"

Cavanaugh smiled. "I heard you had a pretty accurate bullshit detector."

Kelly smiled, as if to say, Well, you heard right. Cavanaugh gestured with his head to a chair and Kelly nodded, allowing it.

Cavanaugh sat. "So I'll get right to the point. Seventeen years ago, I headed up an investigation on the death of Sebastian Deardon."

"A tragic . . . accident," Kelly said, curiously, sitting herself.

"That's what it says in my official report, but that's not what I wrote. I called it murder then . . . I'm calling it murder now."

Kelly paused a minute. Then she leaned forward in her seat. "Are you saying that someone higher up changed the record, altered the facts?"

"I'm saying rich people have powerful friends. I'm saying seventeen years ago, I pushed that case with the Captain and suddenly I'm busting winos on Staten Island. Somebody put that schneid on my whole damn career, and C. J. Cavanaugh never forgets."

Kelly looked at the big man, trying to figure him. "If you're asking for sympathy, you've got it. But why pick me?"

"When I heard they collared the Deardon girl and you were the defense, I figured there'd be a chance to open up the investigation again. Finally get at the truth."

"The charges against Chelsea were dropped, Cavanaugh. Officially, there's nothing left to investigate."

Cavanaugh smiled a little. "Maybe yes . . . maybe no. That's why I came to see you. And give you this . . ."

He dropped the heavy folder on a table in front of her. She looked down at it, then back up at him.

Cavanaugh was rising. "You don't want to know where or how I got that, Miss Kelly, but I think you'll find it interesting reading—a friendly push, you might say."

"If this is stolen merchandise . . ."

"Then you couldn't have got it from me—because we never met, okay? I got eight months to go before I draw my pension. Eight months left to show the Department a clean nose so I can pick up some chump change for the rest of my life. Well, they owe me more than that, Miss Kelly. They owe me satisfaction."

Cavanaugh's voice had turned solemn. Suddenly, he flashed a friendly smile again. "You lay off the white sugar, okay? Stuff'll drop you dead in your tracks."

He winked at her. Then smiling, moving slowly, Cavanaugh was gone.

Kelly circled around the folder for a minute, afraid to touch it. Then she could not resist. Just as she might a piece of candy, she grabbed it and tore it open.

Chapter Ten

That morning was a typical one at One Hundred Centre Street: the building was packed with the usual collection of jurors, judges, lawyers and felons, all moving at lightning speed to make or avoid some appointment with the law.

The only thing missing, Kelly thought, was Tom Logan.

She looked through the crowd of bustling suspects and solicitors and didn't see the familiar scurrying blonde figure anywhere. Clutching Cavanaugh's file to her chest, she scanned the floor, desperately.

Ahead of her, she saw a large attorney—he'd never win a case at that weight and in that suit, she thought—who she remembered knew Logan. She caught up to him.

"Watson," she said, "have you seen Tom Logan?"

"Not since he buried me in court last week," he said, sourly, "and I'm not looking for him, either."

The large attorney lumbered away at a surprisingly rapid pace. Kelly turned and ran alongside a familiar, frantic figure then.

"McHugh," she said, "where's Logan?"

"I'm late!" he screamed. "I'm unprepared! I'm doomed! Goodbye!"

He tried to fly away from Kelly but Kelly held on. She found herself being dragged down the hall with him.

"I need Logan!" she shouted.

"Courtroom seven!" he finally told her. "No, six! One of them! Let me go!"

Kelly did. McHugh darted into the huge, ever-moving crowd that was trying to administer or elude justice. Kelly went to find Logan, her fingers gripping the file as if for dear life. And it would mean someone's life: Chelsea Deardon's.

She found him in courtroom seven, in the midst of prosecuting a case. Logan was standing very seriously opposite a witness, a flashily dressed woman of forty. Kelly moved quickly down the aisle towards him.

"Is it not true," Logan was saying, "that you were having sexual relations with the defendant *before* the crime was committed?"

Kelly began clearing her throat loudly as she walked. Soon she was a veritable symphony of mucous discomfort. But Logan continued, lost in the drama of his questioning.

"No," the woman answered him.

Logan made a dramatic half-turn to the judge. On his way round, he saw a woman making a frantic high sign at him from the aisle. And not just any woman, either.

Logan was completely distracted by the suddenness of seeing Kelly. His voice lost its decisiveness.

"I see . . ." he said. "Then you don't deny it."

"On the contrary," the woman said, "I just did deny it."

Kelly was signaling him with her eyes. They were shooting a desperate message: "Come over here!" Logan tried manfully to direct his attention back to the witness.

"Oh. Now then, Mrs. Wilson . . ."

"Williams," the woman said.

Kelly's face was turning a kind of purple color, as if her hands were around her own throat, choking her. He looked back, confusedly, to the woman on the stand.

"I beg your pardon?" he said.

"My name is Williams. Mrs. Wilson is the wife of the defendant."

"Well, of course she is," Logan said, definitively. "You're absolutely right."

The Judge, who had heretofore seemed to be drifting into sleep, was awakened. He glanced curiously at Logan. Then he looked where Logan was looking: at the purple, gesticulating Kelly. He cleared his throat.

"Miss Kelly," he said, "today is my birthday, and things have been going so well for me. Are you going to spoil my birthday?"

Kelly was thrilled at this invitation to finally speak. She strode confidently closer to the bench.

"Begging the court's indulgence," she said, "if I might confer with Mr. Logan for a moment . . ."

"Now?" the Judge said, incredulously. "Right now?"

"It really won't take more than a moment, Your Honor."

The Judge turned with terrifying slowness to the Assistant District Attorney. "Mr. Logan?"

"I have no objection," Logan said, sighing. Then he turned to the witness. "With apologies to Mrs. . . ."

"Williams," the woman told him. "Oh, I don't mind."

The Judge looked over at Kelly, who was nodding, hopefully. Then he looked back at Logan, who was nodding, fatalistically. Then he looked back at Kelly again, who was smiling, sweetly at him, as if he had already said yes. Then he exploded.

"Well then, get on with it!"

Exasperatedly, the Judge banged his gavel. Like a runner out of the starting gate, Logan sprang to the sidelines.

Kelly leaned in close to him. He was surprised at how glad he was to see her. He had been bottling up the whole incredible story of the night before; he had been waiting to tell her.

Kelly grinned, expectantly. She was surprised at how glad she was to see him. She was fit to burst with her incredible find of that morning; she had been waiting to tell him.

"I called you last night," Logan whispered. "Something incredible happened."

"I'll say it did," Kelly said, "I made a huge discovery in . . . you called me last night?"

"Yes. What huge discovery?"

"The Deardon case," she told him. "Major fraud. I have *hard evidence.*"

Logan couldn't help it; he felt his heart beat faster at this news. He wanted to hear about it more than anything else—certainly more than this case.

He turned. "Your Honor, a very important matter has come up which demands my immediate attention. My learned assistant, Ms. Freeman, will continue the cross-examination in my absence."

Logan looked over at the prosecution table, where Freeman was sitting. Instinctively, the young woman jumped up. "What? Me?"

Logan met her question with an encouraging nod. Then he followed Kelly quickly up the aisle and out the door. Behind him, the only sounds he heard were Freeman's protests and the Judge's sighs.

Logan and Kelly came out into the corridor. They kept walking and spoke in excited whispers.

"Somebody took a shot at me last night," he told her, "right in front of Chelsea's place."

"Shot at . . . ?"

"I've arranged a twenty-four hour stakeout on her."

"Chelsea's place?" Kelly's voice had an edge on it now. "What were you doing at Chelsea's place?"

"I couldn't sleep, and . . . it's a long story."

"I have time."

"Later. Let's see the hard evidence."

The two of them glided into Logan's office. They went right past Doreen, who jumped up, holding messages, but to no avail. Immediately, they were behind the closed door of Logan's inner office.

Kelly cleared a place on Logan's cluttered desk. Then she laid the file down on it. From it, she removed a photograph album. On the cover was printed: Seaboard Fidelity—File D-10623428—Deardon, Sebastian.

Logan just looked at it for a minute.

"Open it," Kelly said.

Slowly, Logan did. He discovered a series of photographs of Deardon's paintings. He flipped through them. Each had been painstakingly numbered, titled and dated.

"It's the complete collection of Sebastian Deardon's paintings," Kelly said.

Logan knew it was more than that. "This is a confidential insurance file. Where did you get this?"

"I have my sources," Kelly said, proudly. "See the red stamps next to most of the paintings? Those were the ones that were destroyed in the fire. Now, look at painting number one-twenty-two."

Logan flipped the pages. He stopped at the appropriate painting.

"Look familiar?" Kelly asked.

Logan shrugged. "They all look about the same to me."

Kelly stared at him in disbelief. Logan looked a bit more carefully at it. He cleared his throat, abashedly.

"Okay, this looks like the painting Taft showed us at the gallery," he said.

"Not looks like, Logan—*is*. Take my word for it. Notice the red stamp next to it? That painting was supposedly destroyed in the fire."

Logan looked up, very slowly, from the painting. He saw that Kelly was staring at him, heatedly, as if she too were burning up.

They wasted no time.

Chapter Eleven

Taft's assistant, Roger, had not wanted to tell them where his boss was. Logan, however, made it sound so urgent over the phone that the loyal underling at last gave in. Taft would be at an auction at Sotheby's that night.

The famous auction house was located at Seventy-second Street and York Avenue. It took up almost the entire block and its huge glass windows gave it an air of disdain. That night, Logan pulled his car up right outside.

He and Kelly entered and made straight for the auction room. As they glided silently over the plush carpets, they whispered urgently to each other.

"I say we squeeze him and see what comes out," Kelly said.

Logan shook his head. "We're going to go slow with this guy. I don't want to hear the word 'fraud' come out of your mouth. We don't know what we've got. It could be a clerical error."

"Right. A twenty million dollar clerical error."

"Look, I'm here without any authority whatsoever. You're in possession of insurance files of totally dubious origin."

They stopped at the auction door.

"Inside I do the talking," Logan said. "You just stand behind me and try to look like an attorney."

Kelly smirked. "Of course, Your Holiness."

Logan smirked back. Then the two of them entered the room.

The place was packed with wealthy buyers, sellers, collectors and connoisseurs from all over the world. Their dress was immaculate, their manners impeccable. Right at this instant, they sat rapt as bidding began on a painting.

The bidding was begun by Taft.

He looked just as suave, implacable and slightly dangerous as he had the time before. He had only slightly raised a finger but with the gesture, he had said: I can afford this painting and I will own it.

Logan and Kelly stealthily moved to the back row, where Taft sat. Then as quietly as they could, they slipped into the seats beside him.

Taft turned. He was obviously startled but after a second of shock, he brilliantly disguised it. He gave them a pursed little smile.

"Mr. Taft," Logan whispered, "we'd like to ask you a few more questions about that Deardon painting if we may."

"Actually," he whispered back, "I'm in the middle of pursuing a rather illusive painting, so I'm afraid . . ."

"I'm really sorry to bother you," Logan continued earnestly, "but a colleague of mine received some documents related to some art underwriting that was done by the Seaboard Fidelity Corporation . . ."

This gentle prodding hit its mark. Taft's voice began to reveal tell-tale traces of anger. "Please. Can't you see I'm busy right now?"

Kelly jumped in then. "We've found evidence indicating that

not as many Deardon paintings were destroyed in that fire as was previously thought." Here she paused. "In fact, maybe none were."

Taft gave a slight twitch. Then suddenly, he stood. He walked to the back of the auction room. As they followed, Logan shot Kelly a warning glance. Go easy, it said.

Taft spoke then, obviously restraining himself. "I was there that night, you know. I carried little Chelsea out through the flames. I saved her life. Everything else—*everything*—burned to the ground."

This confession had meant to shame them out of their suspicions. But Kelly pressed fearlessly on.

"Remember that Deardon you showed us yesterday?" she asked. "Well, somehow, it managed to survive."

Taft blew up then. His voice went from whisper to shout and took them both by surprise.

"That's it!" he said. "Get out, both of you, before I have you thrown out."

Logan glanced around them, cautiously. He held up a hand to calm Taft. "Look, Mr. Taft, we're not here to make specific charges . . ."

"We know the Deardon paintings still exist," Kelly said. "We think you have those paintings."

There was a pause. Logan stared, miserably, at Kelly. He wished he could have sold *her* at that moment.

Taft completely calmed. His face went blank. His voice turned to ice.

"If you repeat that allegation," Taft said, "anywhere, publicly or privately, I'll see to it that you never practice law in any court in this country."

Taft then gave up on communicating altogether. He looked over to where two uniformed guards were standing. With a wave of his manicured hand, he began to motion them over.

"That won't be necessary," Logan said, quickly, noticing. "I apologize for Ms. Kelly's allegations, but as you know, I represent the District Attorney's office and I *do* intend to have a look at your business records. If you'll cooperate, I'm sure we can avoid any further unpleasantness."

Taft turned all his attentions on Logan then, completely ignoring Kelly. "You seem to be an intelligent man, Mr. Logan. Don't throw away a long and profitable career by meddling into legitimate matters which are none of your concern. Am I making myself clear?"

This attempt at cameraderie and coercion served only to anger Logan.

"Perfectly," he said. "I'll have a subpoena ready in the morning. I want to see *all* your business records for the past five years. Inventories, shipping records, bills of sale—the works. If you fail to comply, a Federal Marshal will confiscate those records and you'll be subject to arrest. Is that clear? Goodbye, Mr. Taft."

"And good luck," Kelly threw in.

She just kept glaring at the older man as she followed the quickly exiting Logan from the room.

As was their wont after matters of investigation, Logan and Kelly came out of Sotheby's with completely opposite reactions. Logan was fuming; Kelly was beaming.

" 'We know those paintings exist,' " Logan said, in a falsetto imitation of Kelly. " 'And we think you have them.' Didn't you learn anything in law school?"

Kelly was totally oblivious. She moved her fists around, as if raring up for another bout. "We really shook him up, didn't we? And that look in your eye at the end—pure, blue steel. God, I'd like to develop a look like that."

Was that how his eyes looked? Logan couldn't help but be complimented. He gave her his expertise. "You don't develop looks. You just . . . look."

"Not me. I practice looks in the mirror. Here's one I picked up from you, by the way. Watch the left brow. I'm cross-examining someone and he gives me an answer I don't buy. Here's how you do it."

Kelly stopped in the middle of the block. She raised her left eyebrow, skeptically. She squinted her eyes into pure, blue steel.

Logan couldn't help himself, he laughed out loud. For the moment, he forgot Kelly's complete breach of legal ethics. They began to walk again.

"Come on, I don't do that," he said.

"All the time," Kelly insisted. "You stand there and sort of make a quarter turn toward the jury with that exact look. You totally discredited Van Dyke with it."

"The Van Dyke case. You were in the courtroom?"

Kelly shrugged. "Some people go to ball games. I go to court. You're the best show in town."

What do you know about that, Logan wondered. He was inspiring. He kind of liked the idea of having a fan. For the moment, he also forgot how much Kelly had exasperated him all the time he had known her.

Then they reached the car, and Logan realized he had forgotten something else: his keys.

Logan did not want Kelly to know. He kept smiling politely at her as his fingers dived wiggling to the bottom of his pockets. Finally he asked, casually,

"Did I give you my car keys?"

"Logan," Kelly said, "I just gave you three major compliments. Meaningful, life-affirming compliments. And—"

"Sorry," Logan said, distracted, searching, "I owe you one . . . Now where . . ."

Kelly shook her head at his lack of enthusiasm. She tried the door to his car. It was locked. She leaned over and peered through the window. Then she straightened up and gave Logan a withering look.

"Logan?" she asked, courteously.

Logan looked up, twisted around from the effort of combing his torso for keys. "What?"

Kelly pointed a thumb towards the sealed window. Logan slowly bent to look inside.

His keys were dangling from the ignition.

Logan looked very slowly and reluctantly back at Kelly. Her eyes had narrowed now into judgmental slits. She seemed to be saying, And this is the man on whom I lavished so much praise.

Logan immediately affected a confident air. "No problem," he said, frowning indifferently. "I've done this before."

Then he quickly ran away from Kelly, across the street.

Logan didn't go home and he didn't cut over to a side street to hail a cab. He flew right back through the front doors of Sotheby's.

Once inside, he slowed to an inconspicuous walk. He sauntered over to the coat room. He politely asked the woman working there for a wire hanger. She looked at him witheringly—Sotheby's used wood. Then she shrugged and reached below her table and brought one out. Logan grinned.

Whistling, he strolled as cavalierly as anyone could carrying a wire hanger. Then he saw something that made him stop altogether.

He saw Victor Taft.

Taft was in a phone booth, with his back to Logan. But his head and shoulders were bobbing so excitedly, his entire body was so animated, that it was clear his conversation was urgent. Logan watched him for a while. Then with his hanger, he made a suave exit from Sotheby's and went to break into his own car.

The trick was first to straighten out the hanger. Kelly watched with a certain amount of appalled fascination as Logan did so, right in front of her, in clear view of passersby.

"May I ask what you're doing?" she said.

"A little trick I picked up while prosecuting car thieves," Logan explained.

Logan proceeded to bend the end of the straightened hanger into an "L" shape. Then with the seriousness of a surgeon, he slowly pushed it into the narrow space between the door glass and the rubber window casing.

"Here," Logan said, as if asking for scalpels, "push on the window."

With great misgivings, Kelly gave him an assist. She pushed both of her hands hard against the window. Meanwhile, Logan fished for the inside door latch with the hooked end of the hanger.

"Like this?" Kelly asked.

"Good," Logan answered.

As the operation continued, both the doctor and his assistant came in close contact. Their cheeks brushed slightly against each other's. Their shoulders touched; the sides of their thighs tensed one against the other.

Kelly did nothing to discourage the proximity. But Logan threw out a few benign and conscientious words to bring them back to business.

"It isn't always easy to get it," he mumbled, "at first . . ."

But in order to successfully complete the procedure, he had to twist himself even closer to Kelly. Their lips now were nearly together. He could smell the very faint scent of her perfume—nice, he thought, whatever it was. Whichever way he turned, it seemed, his eyes would catch sight of hers. He did not know if he would be able to stop himself from—

The button lock popped up; the door opened.

Both of their attentions went immediately to getting in the car and continuing the case. The only evidence of anything else was the slightly labored sound of their breathing.

"All right," Logan said, "let's go."

"Right," Kelly answered.

Something distracted them then, and it was not any attraction to each other. It was Victor Taft coming out of Sotheby's.

He was walking at a hurried pace. He was shaking his head, very agitatedly. He headed up the sidewalk to his car, a green Mercedes.

"He looks very nervous," Kelly said.

"He is," Logan nodded.

Taft got in quickly. He pulled out jerkily from the curb and zoomed his way into traffic.

Logan and Kelly looked at each other. Neither thought of any other option than of tailing him.

Chapter Twelve

Taft immediately sped off of York and went West. Logan tried to match his speed but traffic and lights kept deterring him. Kelly was no great help, either.

"Don't lose him, Logan," she coached him.

"I'm not going to lose him," Logan said, testily. "Where'd he go?"

Kelly sighed. "South on Second."

Logan took a fast right turn onto Second. Suddenly, on the broad and car-ridden Avenue, Taft's tail lights just seemed to blend into many others. Logan began to sweat. So did Kelly.

"Which one is he?" she asked.

"It was a green Mercedes," Logan answered.

Kelly sighed and beat a frustrated fist upon the dashboard. She peered instantly through the windshield as if trying to find their way in a blizzard. Suddenly, she pointed.

"There! That's him! Change lanes, quick!"

Logan turned to her. "I can't change lanes quick. That thing beside me is called a bus."

As usual, Kelly could not take no for an answer. She shot Logan a glance that challenged everything from his driving skills to his manhood to his parentage. Logan had no choice but to go for it.

He gunned the accelerator. His car shot feverishly ahead of the bus, then made a sharp cut in front of it. The bus' abrasive horn blared into his ear; so did the horns of many other cars around them. But the reckless tactic paid off.

Taft's car was right in front of them.

So was a yellow light. Taft scooted under it just as the light shifted quickly to red. Logan cursed and began to place his foot on the brake.

"Run the light!" Kelly cried. "Run it!"

Logan complied. Sucking in his breath, he switched his foot quickly over to the accelerator. He floored it. The red light became just a tiny spark whizzing past his eyes and disappearing in the rearview.

Kelly was jumping up and down in her seat. She pointed again.

"He's switching to the left lane! Don't let him spot us. Get behind that cab, so we can . . ."

This was too much for Logan. As instinctively as he had sped up, now he instinctively stopped.

He jammed on the brakes. He brought the car to a dead halt in the middle of Second Avenue. Screeching accommodations were made to avert collisions for blocks behind them.

"*Now* what are you doing?" Kelly cried, in exasperation.

Taft's car was tantalizingly close, stopped at a light only a half-block up ahead. Logan did not care. He opened his door and got out in the middle of the street.

A symphony of honking and yelling now surrounded them. Kelly leaned over from her seat to speak out the driver's door.

"Logan," she said, "get back in the car."

"No," he said, obdurately. "I don't want to get back in the car. You drive."

Suddenly, all the ramifications of his actions had been brought home to him. A man who might soon be New York District Attorney speeding down a crowded avenue, breaking traffic laws left and right, to pursue a client who had dropped his case. Besides, it had irked him no end to keep obeying Kelly.

He turned and looked at her. She had a face at once beseeching and infuriated. He stared back, unyielding.

Kelly gave a deep sigh, audible even over the blaring car horns. Then she threw up her hands, as if giving up to him her most humiliating secret.

"I . . . can't drive," she said.

Logan's eyes slowly widened. But the news did not make him madder; instead it made him a bit giddy.

"You've been offering all this expert automotive advice," he said, dryly, "and you *can't drive?*"

Kelly immediately returned to her usual confident tone. "Who needs to know how to drive in New York City?"

For once, being convinced of her rectitude was not going to sway her opponent. Kelly had no choice but to become that most hated of all things: vulnerable.

"The light's changing," she said, in a small voice. "Please . . .?"

The word was a revelation coming from Kelly's mouth. It sounded like a phrase from an obscure foreign language in which she was— to Logan's shock—secretly fluent. It was all he needed to hear.

Logan got back in and closed the door. Kelly scrunched down in the seat beside him.

"The light just changed," she said.

Logan sighed, deeply. Then he gunned the thing.

Chapter Thirteen

Taft kept driving. Logan and Kelly kept driving, too.

They did not stop driving until they had gone much farther downtown, taken an exit, and crossed the Brooklyn Bridge. It was only at the Brooklyn docks that Taft finally reached his destination.

He pulled up outside a large warehouse. Logan kept his car at a cautious distance and killed his lights. He and Kelly sat there in the dark as before them, Taft parked his car and got out.

Taft then climbed up onto the loading dock. He opened an alarm box and inserted a key into it. Then he punched a series of numbers into the code box.

Immediately, the red alarm light went off. A green light came on. And the door to the loading dock began to rise.

Kelly and Logan watched as Taft walked over and disappeared inside. There was a pause. The door remained invitingly open.

"Let's . . ." Kelly began.

"Don't say it," Logan cut in. "I know you've got a lot of 'energy and enthusiasm,' and maybe it hasn't all been bad, but if we go through that door, it's called breaking and entering."

"We're not breaking anything. We're just entering. There's no law against entering."

"There are hundreds of laws against entering."

"Not when you're a government official in pursuit of a felon."

"Felon—no. Not a felon. Not yet, anyway."

Kelly sighed. Then she began to recite, as if speaking to someone dim. "In pursuit of a *probable* felon. Boston versus Cavalero, 1967. If a certified public official is in pursuit of a probable felon, he may enter an unlocked business or storage area without a warrant if he has reasonable suspicion of unlawful activities inside."

For a minute, Logan had to admit he doubted his own memory. Then he just looked irritatedly at Kelly. "Boston versus . . . what a crock . . ."

But Kelly was already out of the car. Through the windshield, he saw her small figure striding confidently for the loading dock. He couldn't just let her go in alone. Logan sighed. Cursing Kelly and his own sense of chivalry, he got out himself.

Trying to run as quietly as he could, he caught up to Kelly at the dock.

"An open door is practically an invitation," Kelly whispered to him. "I really *can* cite cases where an implied invitation is a valid reason to enter."

"In a building with a security system," Logan countered, "implication laws are invalid."

Kelly turned, suddenly. "Wait a minute—did you hear something? Was that Taft?"

She listened again. Then she called in, quietly, "Yes, Victor, coming. Be right there."

Smiling, Kelly slipped into the warehouse. After a second, she poked her head out at Logan.

"He invited you in, too," she said.

Logan rolled his eyes with dismay. Once you start destroying your career, he thought, it's hard to stop. He followed Kelly inside.

The warehouse was cavernous and filled with crates, boxes, bins and lockers used to store art. All the receptacles gave the two of them enough camouflage to move a greater distance inside. Staying low, bobbing from crate to crate, they peered about, looking for Taft. They looked into some of the boxes, but all of them seemed to be empty.

Suddenly, Kelly stopped. She signaled silently for Logan to come over. When he had, she pointed to a locker.

A name was stenciled on it: "Deardon."

Carefully, Logan tried to force the locker open. The door came his way easily; it was unlocked. It was also completely empty.

They continued their darting farther into the stomach of the warehouse. Then they reached a clearing in the center. It was there they stopped.

A giant forklift was stationed there. There did not seem to be sign of anything—or anyone—else. Then they looked over to the right and saw Taft.

He was standing near a row of filing cabinets. With his back to them, he was quickly emptying his briefcase into one of the cabinet drawers. He finished. Then he turned around.

Logan and Kelly quickly ducked. Taft began walking back their way. Soon he passed them. They heard his footsteps slowly fading behind them. Logan swiveled about.

Taft was at the door of the warehouse. He was punching numbers into an interior code box. In a second, the door started closing.

"Oh, great . . ." Logan said.

Taft stepped slowly outside. The door closed behind him.

It shut with a thud that seemed deafeningly final to Logan. He looked over at Kelly. His eyes said, What do we do now?

But Kelly was already up and about. She was moving quickly to the cabinet which Taft had recently left. She was busy pulling open the drawers.

"I hate to blur your concentration," Logan said, "but we're locked in here, you know."

Kelly was busy rifling the drawers. "Spring the door with your coat hanger."

Logan surveyed the huge warehouse for any possible areas of escape. Finding none, he felt panic begin to come over him. He looked back at Kelly. She was deep inside the second drawer.

"Bingo!" she said then. "These are the business records we wanted."

Logan moved swiftly over to where Kelly was investigating. He looked over her shoulder. Kelly pulled the file out to examine it more closely. Logan picked up where she left off, searching the drawer.

"Look at this," Kelly said, excitedly. "Papers of incorporation, dated nineteen sixty-two. A three-man partnership."

Logan took it and read. "Triad Enterprises. Investment Counseling. Victor Taft, Joseph Brock, and Robert Forrester."

"Taft and Forrester were business partners."

"No wonder they traded that painting so quickly," Logan said.

Kelly was ruffling through the rest of it. "Deardon's name is everywhere."

"Joseph Brock—what the hell happened to *him?*"

"His name disappears after nineteen sixty-seven."

Logan pulled another sheet. "Here's the insurance payoff on Deardon's paintings. Taft and Forrester were co-beneficiaries."

Kelly's fingers were still moving inside the drawer. "What is that noise?" she said. "Is that your watch? It's driving me crazy."

Now her fingers suddenly stopped. They had come up against a hard, cold object that seemed wrapped in wires.

She slowly pulled back the folders placed against it. She caught her breath.

"Oh, my God," she said.

It was a time bomb. It clearly read: seventy seconds before detonation.

Chapter Fourteen

Kelly pointed speechlessly at the device. Logan looked over, casually, as if for more business revelations. When he saw the thing, he turned pale.

"Don't touch it," he said. "Leave it alone."

"Logan!" Kelly cried. "Turn it off! *Do* something!"

Logan immediately ran to the warehouse door. He frantically pressed the door lift. There would be no opening it without the alarm code.

Then the alarm went off.

Bells and sirens cried out all over the place. His head hammered by them, Logan ran over to a window. It and all others like it were covered by a strong wire mesh.

Kelly was beside him now. They could hear the screams of the alarm; they felt, too, they could hear the ticking of the bomb. I can't die without seeing my daughter, Logan thought. I can't die before I become D.A. And I'm not so sure I want to die with Laura Kelly.

Swiftly, his attention was taken by the largest object in the warehouse. The forklift. Logan looked at it; then he looked at Kelly. The two of them said nothing. They were too busy running to board it.

Nothing to it, Logan thought, as he got on. Just like a stick shift car. A stick shift car with a giant neck for picking up huge objects; a stick shift car that could bolt crazily out of control.

Before he knew it, he had started it. Before he knew it, they were moving, Logan desperately kicking the gas and jerking the clutch. They were lurching fast towards the only possible exit: the giant warehouse door, which was shut and locked.

The door was a million miles away. Then suddenly, it was two inches from their faces. Then they and the forklift and the door had, in one shattering collision, merged.

Wood and steel flew all over them as they burst through; the impact hurled them back in their seats and sent the machine itself chugging and shaking maniacally. They careened into the outside air.

Then the Earth was rocked by a giant blast.

The bomb had gone off behind them, sending the forklift forward with a wild momentum all its own. There was no stopping it; the thing just went, heading for the only place it could conceivably stop: the river.

The sound of the explosion echoed in their ears; the sounds of fire and chaos raged behind them. The forklift rolled mightily onward, Kelly digging her fingers into Logan's arm, Logan spinning his hands uselessly around the machine's steering wheel.

It sailed right into the river. Logan and Kelly went flying off.

The forklift kept rolling, even in water. Then, finally, it drowned; and after a few more feeble steps, it just floated.

They were underwater a second. Then suddenly, each of them bobbed up above the water's surface. Coughing, cursing and spitting, they swam the short distance in the filthy water back to shore.

Breathing heavily, they walked up the small slope of the embankment. Then the two of them just sat. Each was bruised from top to toe; their head and hands were scratched, stabbed and caked with filth.

Logan looked over at Kelly. Her slight, soaked body was shivering. She was still coughing, deeply. After a second, she subsided.

"You gonna make it?" Logan asked, quietly.

Kelly turned to him. Her soiled face was lighted by the warehouse blaze behind them. She took a deep breath.

"I swear, Logan," she said. "I'll never criticize your driving again."

Chapter Fifteen

Logan and Kelly found out how the other half lived.

They were brought into the Manhattan South police station drenched, bruised, possibly even scarred. And still they were grilled, hounded, photographed and shunted callously from one place to another. Finally, when some magical word seemed to have "come down," they were let go. They were even allowed to keep the blankets they had been given to warm themselves.

The two of them strolled down the packed corridor of the station, dodging cops, reporters and other "criminals." Neither could keep away a little grin at having been through an ordeal and, with ingenuity, survived. They even liked the idea of being suspects—for a few minutes, anyway.

Freeman had come down to pick them up. What she found were not the diligent D.A. for whom she worked or the persistent young Defense Attorney well known at one hundred Centre Street; she found instead two strangely smiling accident victims, adorned with small bandages, some covered with orange ointment, still slightly wet, still slightly shivering. She followed them out perplexedly to the waiting car.

"I'd better warn you," she told Logan, "the Chief is totally crazed—scarfing down those little pink pills like they were M and Ms. He almost let the police charge you and Kelly with breaking and entering."

Suddenly, the prospect of facing Bower's wrath did not upset Logan; he had been becalmed by his ordeal. He turned amused to Kelly.

"I guess he never heard of Boston versus . . ."

"Cavalero," she said, shivering, "nineteen sixty-seven . . ."

"Right . . ." Dazed, Logan looked at Freeman, as if trying to remember who she was. Then he did. "Say, how'd that trial wind up? Did you win it?"

"I'd rather not discuss it, thank you," Freeman said, snippily. "I'll get your car."

She peeled away from the two of them with an addled wave. Logan waved bemusedly back. Then he and Kelly turned a corner.

They passed into an even greater crowd of police, detectives, suspects and press, each moving faster than the other, each screaming louder. They managed to criss-cross their way to the front door.

Then Kelly saw someone she knew.

Logan did not recognize him. He was a big, middle-aged blonde man walking through the station house with ease and a sense of destination. Kelly called to him.

"Cavanaugh! Cavanaugh!"

The man with the insistent knock and the fateful file turned, slowly. When he recognized Kelly, he grinned, broadly.

"Hey, Miss Kelly," he said, approaching. "I was just coming down to see you. Heard all about it." He looked with concern at Kelly's bandaged face. "Jesus . . . must've been a hell of a bang . . ."

Kelly sighed, "I was somewhat luckier than Taft's business records."

"Yeah, well, maybe it could have been somebody trying to blow Taft up, did you think about that? Maybe it was . . ."

Logan was listening with great interest. He had nearly leaned right between Cavanaugh and Kelly. The bigger man noticed; he looked at Logan with an affronted expression.

"I'm talking to the lady here," he said.

"I can see that," Logan said, calmly. "I'm listening to you talking to the lady here."

Cavanaugh turned to Kelly. "Who is this guy?"

Logan turned to Kelly, too. "Who's he?"

Kelly had to smile; she felt as if she were being fought over, and it felt kind of nice, even if it involved possible arson and murder.

"Detective C. J. Cavanaugh," she said, "this is Tom Logan, Assistant District Attorney."

Cavanaugh had heard of him. "Logan? . . . Yeah, sure . . . you got a good rep."

He extended his hand and Logan shook it.

"Tell us about this partnership," Kelly prodded him. "Taft, Forrester . . . and someone named Brock."

"How would he . . ." Logan began.

Kelly cut him off, proudly. "My sources, remember?" Then she announced magnanimously to Cavanaugh, "He can listen in."

Logan parodied an appreciative face. Kelly was oblivious; so was Cavanaugh.

"Not much to tell," he was saying, "on the surface that is. Near as I can figure, the three of them were keeping phony tax records until Taft and Forrester set up Joe Brock to take the fall for it. Brock was sitting in the can at Attica when Deardon was murdered."

"Where's Brock now?" Logan asked.

"He got the Big C the year he was released. Dead and buried in Kansas City, nineteen sixty seven."

"The year his name dropped from those records," Kelly kindly reminded Logan.

Cavanaugh nodded. "Taft kept his gallery, Forrester went into real estate development and . . . that's it. Anyway . . ." he looked around, furtively, "that's where all the right people seem to want it to stop."

"What about Forrester?" Logan asked.

"Very cagey. I could never get a handle on Forrester but I think he's capable of anything. He's very well placed."

Cavanaugh suddenly checked his watch. Then he reached into his wallet, took out a business card and handed it to Logan.

"I gotta get back to my office," he said. "That's my home phone on the bottom. Use it. This case is dead as far as the department is concerned—but I'm counting on you two to keep it alive."

Logan looked at the large man, Cavanaugh. He played it a little like an old movie tough guy, he thought; he was either innocent or he was lying. Logan did not think he was lying.

He shook Cavanaugh's hand again.

Logan and Kelly came out of the station house together. As they took the stairs, he noticed she was limping from the adventure. He could not help it, he felt proud of her then and a little protective.

He wondered what Kelly was doing that evening. Then he re-membered suddenly what *he* was doing: seeing Jennifer. But there was no reason, he considered, why that had to be prohibitive.

"Look," he said, "you hungry? I'm having dinner with my daughter tonight. You're welcome to join us."

"I'm sorry," Kelly replied. "But I almost forgot—I have a date."

Logan was surprised. "A what?"

"A date. You know, like when a man invites you out somewhere for a good time."

This information disturbed Logan, but he kept his tone one of gentle mockery. "Let me be honest. You're in no condition for a date."

"I'm not?" Kelly was taken aback.

"Absolutely not. Your face is grubby, your hair is wet, you can barely walk. You're a mess."

Kelly sighed. "Remember that compliment you owe me? Now would be a good time."

Logan grinned. He thought as a mess—an intrepid, industrious mess—Kelly looked the most attractive he had ever seen her. He did not think then, he just acted. He placed his hands lightly on either side of Kelly's head; then he slowly and gently brushed back her hair.

"You have the warmest eyes . . . and the coldest ears in town."

They both smiled then. People streamed out around them from the station house, but they might as well have been alone; that was how close they felt. Logan did not move his hands from her hair; Kelly did not move her face away.

"I'm only counting that as half a compliment," she said, teasingly. "That way you're still on the hook."

She pulled slowly from him. Then she started, haltingly, down the stairs by herself.

You're still on the hook, Logan thought. That meant To Be Continued. Just to make sure, he called after her,

"Raincheck on dinner?"

Kelly stopped. She turned back and smiled at him, warmly.

"Raincheck," she answered.

Then she was gone, on her bum leg. Logan watched her disappear into the crowd of other people. She stood out from them, he thought; she always had.

Legal Eagles: Laura Kelly (Debra Winger) and Tom Logan (Robert Redford).

(Top) Chelsea Deardon (Daryl Hannah) and Tom Logan in a Soho bar. (Bottom) Kelly and Logan meet Victor Taft (Terence Stamp) in his gallery.

Chelsea Deardon — performance artist.

Chelsea arrives dishevelled at Logan's apartment (top), then makes herself at home.

An abrupt awakening for Logan and Chelsea as police burst in to arrest her for murder (top), and Logan faces the press.

Logan and Kelly for the Defense: working in Kelly's office (top), and at the Courthouse.

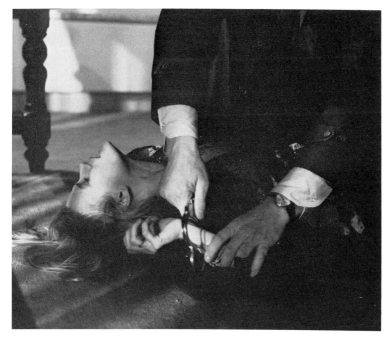

Kelly and Cavanaugh (Brian Dennehy) find the hidden paintings (top), and the terrified Chelsea is immobilized.

Logan searches for Kelly and Chelsea in the Taft Gallery inferno.

Chapter Sixteen

It was another Logan feast for Jennifer.

Take-out Chinese, to be exact, and not very good at that. Jennifer didn't seem to mind. She ate the food ravenously, seeming to enjoy roughing it with Dad. Lousy food, grungy apartment; it meant living the way he did, being close. Every stale noodle was an authentic piece of her father. She did not get enough of those.

Logan could sense the way she felt but *he* still felt bad: it should have been a home-cooked meal. Then he remembered the oatmeal debacle and decided even the Hung Lo Palace was an improvement.

After the meal, he watched as Jennifer thumbed through the huge stacks of legal briefs which were his caseload. She seemed genuinely interested; but maybe she was just a deprived daughter delving into her father's life and not a budding attorney. Either way, it tickled Logan.

"Never be a lawyer," he told her. "No one ever appreciates you."

Jennifer smiled a little, still engrossed. Then as if she had had something on her mind all night, she slowly looked up.

"Dad," she said, "when you get to be District Attorney, does that mean you have to go into politics?"

"I'm already in politics," he replied. "Politics is more than just running for election. Politics is . . ." He tried to reduce the cynical tone sneaking into his voice. "Well, politics *should* be . . . the wise exercise, distribution and maintenance of power."

"Then what's sexual politics?" Jennifer asked then.

Logan was jolted. But he tried to appear the calm, cool, sophisticated modern father. "Sexual politics? Sexual politics. Sure, sexual politics. That's when . . . well, sexual considerations . . ."

Jennifer shot in. "Like when you call a boy and he won't call you 'cause he's too cool so you have to call him to tell him he's cool so he can tell his friends that you like him, but he won't say he likes you?"

Logan slowly cleared his throat, embarrassed. "That's a very precise definition, yes."

"Then politics is just getting what you want, right?"

"Close enough. You're going to be a terrific lawyer, you know that?" He breathed easier. He was very glad Jennifer had answered her own question; he suspected he would have gone straight from hemming and hawing to foolishly pontificating. He thanked Jennifer silently for saving them both from that.

The whole conversation had brought other thoughts into Logan's head. Sex made him think of Laura Kelly, suddenly. It also made him think of Chelsea Deardon. He had a sneaking suspicion he was going to have to choose which one to keep thinking about. For the time being, there was no contest.

"I invited a really terrific lawyer over for dinner tonight," he said, "but unfortunately she couldn't make it."

The doorbell rang then.

Speak of the devil, Logan thought. He had the strange premonition—fueled by hope—that Laura had decided to reconsider after all. That whole date business was probably just to put him off, to take things easy. Who would go out with her, anyway? Who would be better for her than Logan? With a smile, he excused himself to Jennifer and headed for the front door. He opened it.

It was Chelsea.

She was not, however, the Chelsea he had been thinking about. This was a scared, shaking woman, pitiably frail. Her blonde hair had been doused by rain and now stuck to her face and neck. Her whole dress had been soaked through. She looked like a wounded animal that was on the run. Indeed for a minute or so, she could not even make a human noise.

Finally, she said, "I did something really crazy."

Logan should have been sympathetic; he knew that. Yet tonight Chelsea seemed to be just a troubled girl always turning up with some melodramatic announcement. He no longer knew what to believe from her, and he was not so sure he cared to expend the energy. Besides, she was not the girl of his dreams tonight. Besides, there was Jennifer to consider.

"This is not a good time . . ." he said, clearly irritated.

"I went to see Victor Taft," she went on. "I had a gun."

Logan just looked at her. There was no way he could turn her away after those words.

"You . . . better come in," he said.

Chelsea entered, obviously close to hysteria. From back in the apartment, Jennifer perked her head up, with interest. She pointed at the traumatized and disheveled visitor. She mimed, "The lawyer?" Logan rolled his eyes and shook his head, No, for God's sake.

Chelsea was babbling. "I . . . tried to force him to tell me where my father's paintings were."

"With a gun?"

"He called my bluff. Knocked me around, took the gun away . . ." She turned and sure enough there was a blue-purple lump on her cheek. "I got all panicky. I finally managed to break free and ran out."

Logan sighed. "Have you called Kelly?"

"I left a message on her machine."

Right, Logan thought, sourly, she's on a date.

"Listen," Chelsea said, "Victor said he was going to call the police. I could really be in trouble this time."

"All right. Get yourself dried off and find something to wear. I'll try Kelly again and . . ."

Logan had pointed toward the bedroom. In that direction, he saw the smiling, expectant, clearly intrigued face of his only child.

"Oh, Chelsea, I'm sorry," he said, "this is my daughter, Jennifer."

Jennifer thought the whole thing was obviously neat. "Hi."

Chelsea just stared back in silence, shaking, numb. Logan placed his hands reassuringly—but carefully—on her shoulders.

"It'll be all right, do you hear me?" Then he couldn't help himself; Chelsea always had this effect on him. "I'll handle it."

Chelsea managed a nod. Then slowly she entered Logan's bedroom and closed the door behind her.

Jennifer looked at Logan, suspiciously.

"She looks guilty to me," she said.

Logan had to smile. "A juror's supposed to wait until she's heard all the evidence."

"Dad," Jennifer said, cautiously, "is this someone I'm going to get to know real well?"

"Not very well, no. But that doesn't mean you shouldn't be on your best behavior."

Jennifer nodded. Then speaking it seemed for her father's own good, in a small voice, she added,

"You, too, right, Dad?"

Then the doorbell rang again.

Logan and Jennifer exchanged careful glances. What now? Logan thought. Seeing her father was not moving, Jennifer started towards the door.

"Wait," Logan said. "It might be the police."

"Why are we protecting her?" Jennifer asked him, pointedly. "She's your girlfriend, isn't she?"

Logan was adamant. "She's just a client."

The doorbell rang again. Calming himself, Logan crossed to the door. Then he looked back at Jennifer.

"You know what happens to stool pigeons?" he asked, leadingly.

Jennifer nodded, obediently. "People stick their feet in cement and throw them in the river."

"That's right."

Logan winked at her. Then he pulled the door open.

Barbara was standing there.

Logan thought he might have a heart attack. He looked at his ex-wife, who was also wet with rain, and all he could do was smile. A big, crazed, terrified smile.

"Uh—hi!" he spat out. "What a . . . nice surprise. Look, Jennifer, look who's here."

"Hi, Mom," Jennifer said, easily. "We thought you were the cops."

Barbara was clearly in no mood. "I've been parked outside in the rain, blowing the horn for ten minutes."

"Well, she's all ready to go," Logan said, quickly. "Ready to go, Jennifer? She's ready to go."

Barbara looked at her husband, who was making several sweeping gestures with his arms, as if ushering Jennifer out. "What's the matter with you? Why are you . . ."

Barbara got her answer then. It came in the form of a lithe blonde woman.

Chelsea came out of Logan's bedroom, dressed only in Logan's pajama top. She was drying her hair with a towel.

Barbara caught her breath. She looked at Chelsea. Then she looked at Logan. Then she looked at Jennifer. With each look, she grew more stunned.

"Oh, my God . . ." she whispered. Beseechingly, she added, "Not in front of the kid."

Logan sighed. "Nothing happened in front of the kid."

Jennifer piped up. "Dad didn't hit her in the face, Mom. It was some guy she was trying to rob with a gun."

Barbara's eyes grew wider. She turned and stared at Logan, as if to say, How Could You?

Logan could only respond with a disparaging smile. "Now Barbara, I realize this all sounds a bit melodramatic, but . . ."

"Congratulations," she interrupted him. "What a perfect environment for my daughter to grow up in."

"She's *our* daughter. You always seem to forget that."

"Right now, I'm trying very hard to forget that, yes. Come on, Jennifer, let's get out of here."

Barbara said it as if they were fleeing the most base den of iniquity. Fleeing to someplace safe. Beverly Hills, maybe, Logan thought, with chagrin.

Jennifer walked over. But she did not go with her mother right away. First she stopped at Logan. She reached up and gave him a hug.

"Don't worry, Dad," she whispered. "I'll make sure she knows you didn't do anything."

"You're the best thing *I* ever did," he answered, touched.

"I still think she's guilty."

Logan grinned. Barbara quickly took Jennifer's hand and whisked her out the door. He saw a fleeting glimpse of his daughter's waving hand before he saw only wood, the spy-hole, the knob.

Barbara and Jennifer did not see much themselves on their way out to the car. Barbara's eyes were blurred by rage; Jennifer was being pulled too fast to see anything.

They certainly couldn't see the heavyset man standing on the corner, watching Logan's window.

Chapter Seventeen

After his ex-wife and daughter were gone, Logan turned slowly around. For a moment, he believed he was alone. Then he heard the soft scratch of terrycloth against scalp.

He looked over. Chelsea was still drying her hair. She did it mechanically now, as if just trying to occupy herself, just trying to avoid Logan.

She could not avoid him for long. He was staring at her, shaking his head at this turn of events in front of his ex-wife, wondering what in the world he was going to do with her.

"I've screwed things up for you," she said, finally, "haven't I? I'm always doing that."

Logan felt torn between annoyance and empathy now. "Forget it."

Chelsea drew her arms about herself. "I can't seem to stop shaking. Do you have anything?"

Logan shrugged. "Look in the fridge. I'll try Kelly."

She moved to the kitchen and he heard her sadly rustling around. Logan pulled Kelly's number out of his address book. He dialed.

"Hi, this is Laura Kelly," came the answer. "I'm not able to come to the phone right now . . ."

". . . but if you leave your name and number . . ." Logan imitated.

He slammed the phone down. Probably still out on her big date, he thought, peeved. She's probably sitting in a movie by herself, he thought, that's what she's doing. Just didn't want to get in too deep with me.

He turned and saw Chelsea. She was standing in the kitchen doorway, still only dressed in his pajama top. She had her feet crossed, pensively, her head cocked to one side.

What was he going to do? Send her out in the rain? Yet he hesitated. What if her story about the gun was true? How would his harboring her look?

Logan shook his head at himself. Who would ever know?

"Come on," he said, "let's open up the couch."

The two of them threw the pillows to the floor. Then each bent at either end.

"Ready?" Logan said. "One . . . two . . . three!"

The couch seemed to weigh a ton. The two of them barely managed to spread it open upon the floor. Logan just looked at it, curiously.

"I can't understand it," he said. "Jennifer does this with one hand."

Logan went off to get a blanket. He heard Chelsea childishly bouncing on the bed to test it. He returned to find her landing with a bump.

"The first thing tomorrow morning," he told her, "you're calling Kelly. Then you're going to the police and filing a report. Taft may have been bluffing tonight, but I want you to play it safe."

Chelsea pouted. "Why can't you come with me?"

"Why? Why . . ." Logan had to come up with something fast. He did. "Because she's your attorney and I'm not." He lay the blanket on the bed. "Anything else?"

104

"A personal question?"

Logan sighed. "Why not."

"What do you think of me?"

So many words ricocheted through his head; which one to choose? "I think you're . . . interesting."

"A carefully chosen word."

"Carefully chosen words are the tools of my profession."

"The other night, when I kissed you. What did you think about that?"

That's the second personal question, Logan thought, she's already had her allotment. He decided to answer her, anyway.

"Dangerous," he said.

Chelsea smiled, privately. They looked at each other, with what seemed for once like an actual understanding.

"See you in the morning," Logan said.

"See you in the morning."

Logan couldn't sleep again.

He tried his usual repertoire of positions: Christ-like, fetal, et al. He turned to one side, gripping the pillow at his stomach like a football. He sensed that nothing was going to work tonight.

It could have been Chelsea's presence in the other room that kept him up. He should have retained his annoyance at her and not given in to pity, or to attraction. Riding a forklift into the river was one thing; giving Chelsea lodging was just *too* reckless. He could just imagine Laura's face when—or if—he told her.

Laura. She, too, was murdering his sleep. He wondered if she was home from her date by *now*. Or her late movie. Worrying about the two women made him wriggle even more restlessly. He stretched out his arm, flailing to the other, unseen side of the bed.

It touched Chelsea.

Logan slowly turned. She was lying there, staring at him. She was not even wearing his pajama top now.

"Neither could I," she said.

"What . . ." Logan said, startled.

"I couldn't sleep, either."

"When did you . . ."

"A little while ago. It's . . . difficult for you to relax, isn't it?"

"Right now?" he asked, shrilly. "Yes, it is."

Chelsea smiled. She pulled the blanket in closer around them.

"Forget you're a lawyer for a moment," she said. "I came here because I trust you."

She was whispering now. Her mouth was getting nearer and nearer to his. He could feel her bare flesh crushing itself against him.

"And because I'm so alone . . ."

She kissed him then: a long and deep kiss. Logan felt his heart thumping in his ears. He understood the temptations criminals experienced—and succumbed to. He decided to become more than an accessory. He kissed her back.

It had always been just a matter of time.

They met the morning in each other's arms.

To be more exact, they did so wrapped around each other, Logan's arm draped protectively about Chelsea's shoulder, Chelsea's blonde hair mingling with the blonde hair on his chest. The remedy to their restlessness had worked; the two of them slept soundly.

Then the door suddenly flew open.

Four uniformed cops were in the room, their weapons drawn. The sound shocked both of them awake. Chelsea screamed. Logan bolted upright in bed. He was staring at four barrels.

"What the hell . . ." he began.

The cops surrounded the bed then. In their haste, they knocked over a lamp and a table. The crashes seemed to echo all over the neighborhood. The guns drew closer, aimed right at their horrified faces.

The first cop spoke. "You have the right to remain silent. You have the right . . ."

"I know my rights!" Logan thundered at him. "Now what . . ."

He was starting to get up. A second cop grew edgy.

"Freeze!" he shouted. "Don't move again!"

"I'm not moving!" Logan shouted back. "I'm an Assistant D.A., for Chrissake! What the hell . . ."

"Shut up!"

The first cop turned to Chelsea. "Chelsea Deardon—you are under arrest for the murder of Victor Taft."

Logan turned slowly to the shivering girl. He looked at her with total disbelief.

"No!" she cried. "It's not true!"

Harshly, the cops started snapping handcuffs on the startled lovers. Chelsea had to struggle to keep the sheet around herself.

"Anything you say may be held against you," the first cop went on. "You have the right to an attorney . . ."

"Looks like she's already had her attorney," the second cop chuckled.

"Screw you!" Logan said.

It was the only thing he could say. What else can you say when someone takes away your dignity, your reputation and maybe even your future?

Chapter Eighteen

Freeman bailed him out.

She brought him a fresh shirt and jacket. In the bowels of the police station, near the filthy cell where he had spent the day, she also brought him some information.

"It doesn't look good," she said.

Logan nodded. That was the understatement of the decade. For an Assistant D.A. to be found in bed with a beautiful female suspect, no, no, that didn't look good. But Freeman was talking about Chelsea.

"She's being held without bond. The police report says her prints were on the weapon, and there were two witnesses who saw her run out of the apartment."

Logan shook his head. It seemed Chelsea had screwed him more than once last night. Nice use of restraint, Logan, he thought. After this, it was straight to the monastery.

Logan and Freeman passed the other cells in the dank station jail. When they came to a door at the end, Freeman had an additional word of advice.

"Brace yourself," she said.

She threw open the door. The whole world was watching.

At least, it seemed like the whole world. It was really only the entire New York press. At least a dozen reporters and TV cameras attacked him at once. Logan winced as he saw the ocean of inquiry cascade upon him, interrogations resounding in his ears.

"Watch it!" Freeman yelled at them all. "Coming through here . . ."

They did not watch it, of course, or make way. Instead, they all trailed him right to the street. There they were joined by what seemed like the rest of the world press. Logan and Freeman stepped out into an unavoidable mob of media.

"Is it true you were found in bed with the suspect?"

"They're calling you 'The Darling D.A.' What do you think of the name?"

"Our clairvoyant at World People says Chelsea Deardon is carrying your child, Logan. Can we . . ."

"The police report said you were both naked. Do you usually examine suspects that way?"

Logan did not even think. He wheeled around and grabbed the last reporter by the lapels. He started to take a swing right at his face. This will be a "No Comment" he'll never forget, he thought.

But he was stopped. A big man with a familiar face quickly intervened.

C. J. Cavanaugh pushed the reporter back, spun him around, and "accidentally" tripped him into the crowd of his colleagues.

"When you spread crap in this city," Cavanaugh told the supine reporter, "you're supposed to pick it up."

Then he turned to Logan, who was staring at him with as much admiration as surprise. "Follow me, I got a cab waiting."

It wasn't hard to get through the crowd with Cavanaugh blocking. Lucky for me, Logan thought, Cavanaugh came along; assault and battery is an additional charge I don't need.

Cavanaugh raised a big mitt and cabs were too frightened not to stop. One came screeching obediently to the curb. Cavanaugh opened the door for Logan.

"Thanks," Logan said, sincerely.

Cavanaugh nodded. "Calling it quits?"

It was more of a dare than a question.

"Just warming up," Logan answered.

If Cavanaugh's was a face he was glad to see, there was another the sight of which he was dreading: Maxwell Bower's.

The District Attorney did not disappoint him. His face was red, bloated and trembling with rage. He looked with disbelief at the pile of newspapers laid on his desk. Each one had a headline about Logan's escapade. "Love Nest" was used more than once in the headlines; Bower himself was even featured inside, caught rushing miserably to his office.

Logan sat like a schoolboy opposite his boss. He felt he should hold out his hand and wait for the ruler to hit. But he knew he would get more than just a slap.

It was a minute before Bower could stop shaking his head long enough to speak. And when he did, he exploded.

"One year! I had one more year, dammit! And now what do you think they're going to remember—the sixty seven thousand convictions I got? Not on your sweet, sexually active ass, they're not!"

Logan winced. When he was younger, he might have taken a certain amount of pride in this description; today it only made him feel foolish.

"They're going to remember one horny bastard who made my office the laughing stock of the city! Goddamit, Logan, when this office services the community, we do it with our pants on!"

Suddenly, Logan did not feel so sheepish. There were a lot of unanswered questions about the whole incident. His natural sense of self-preservation rose in him then. It was no crime to sleep with a beautiful woman—even if she might be a murderess.

110

"Who sent the cops to my place?" he shot back, equalling Bower's volume. "Who knew Chelsea was there?"

"An anonymous caller," Bower said.

"Most anonymous calls go right in the waste basket, don't they?"

"Most anonymous calls don't involve an assistant district attorney!"

Logan was silent then. This whole thing was beginning to smell. "Somebody set me up. Who was it?"

"Nobody in this office, I damn well know that!"

Bowers got up then. Logan feared his boss might take a swing; he recoiled, instinctively. But Bower was only intending to pace.

"Look, this is an extraordinary breach of ethics. I've got no alternative but to suspend you for ninety days, pending an investigation."

Logan felt his hands roll suddenly into fists at his side. At the same time, he could not stop tears from forming in his eyes.

"Suspend me?" he said. "What the hell kind of cheap political dodge is that? Hey, when I really need your help and support . . . *suspend* me?"

There was a pause. Bower's eyes bulged at Logan, apoplectically. For a minute, Logan thought maybe he had gone too far; yet part of him also felt he was totally within his rights. He expected Bower to chuck him out of his job entirely—and maybe even out the door.

But Bower wasn't angry, not at Logan, anyway. He seemed angry at himself now. He trembled again but with regret.

"You're right," he said. "You're absolutely right. I'm *not* going to suspend you."

Logan smiled and began to express his thanks. Then he saw what words were slowly being formed in Bower's mouth.

"You're . . ."

Logan jumped up. "Stop! I won't accept that."

Bower completed it: ". . . fired!"

Logan felt like tackling the old fool. Maybe he wished he could get a woman as attractive and young as Chelsea. Maybe he was just too far in the pockets of all the powers that be. Either way, Logan felt his respect for his superior evaporate.

He spat out some lines he had heard in numerous old movies but had never—fortunately—had the opportunity to use himself.

"You can't fire me," he shouted. "I quit!"

He felt some satisfaction at uttering the lines; he also felt at best he had won a Pyrrhic victory. He had never had the opportunity to use that expression before, either.

Logan stormed out of the office.

He walked down the packed, active corridors of the Criminal Courts building, cursing constantly to himself. He felt the urge to push anyone before him out of his way. He also felt misery at soon no longer being among them.

As he walked, out of the corner of his eyes, he saw a lean young man walking alongside him. He was out of breath and seemingly relieved at having caught up.

"You're Logan?" the man said.

"Yeah," Logan said, coldly.

"Saw your picture in the paper."

"What about it?" Just one more word, Logan thought, keep talking, I got something for you.

"Nothing. I just think you got a raw deal from the press."

Logan breathed easier. At last, a man with insight. "Thanks."

The man smiled. Then as Logan raised a waving hand and turned to go, the man stuck a paper into his outstretched palm.

It was a subpoena.

"This requires you to appear in court," the man said, "to give cause why you are inhibiting the proper education of your daughter. Your former wife has brought charges before Judge Lloyd Solomon in District Court. You may bring legal counsel for this hearing if you desire."

The man nodded, pleasantly, and walked away. Soon he was lost in the crowd.

Logan looked with disbelief at the paper in his hand. Good going, Barbara, he thought, dig your foot a little harder into my prone body. Still, his anger was mixed with a good amount of fear.

Logan immediately moved to a pay phone. He dropped in a quarter and frantically, furiously, dialed.

"You want to play rough?" he screamed. "You want to find out how Goddamned good a lawyer I am? Well, you got it, sweetheart. I'm going to cut you into so many legal pieces they're going to have to take you home in a paper bag!"

Logan suddenly winced as he heard the response of a small, familiar voice. "Jennifer? Oh, God . . . Hello, darling, could you please put Mom on? No, no . . . everything's fine . . . really . . . I'm just very angry." He could not keep himself from laughing then. "Well, when she gets out of the tub, would you tell her I called? Okay, honey? I love you, too. Bye."

Logan hung up, with a sigh. Then he made his way swiftly to his office, keeping his red face averted.

In his office, the vultures had already descended.

The particular vulture in question was named Blanchard. The proper and humorless young man did not want a numbered form today; he wanted Logan's entire office. He was busy clearing off the many files and papers from Logan's desk.

"Hey!" Logan yelled. "What the hell do you think you're doing in here?"

"You're out, Logan," Blanchard said, emptying out another file. "You're history. This is my office now."

"This is *my* damn office until I clean out my own damn desk!"

Blanchard just looked at Logan, triumphantly. Then with a smug smile, he made his exit—and it was only temporary, he seemed to suggest.

"You wouldn't listen, would you," he chided. "Everything had to be done *your* way . . ."

Blanchard disappeared, like the Ghost of Unemployment Yet-to-Come.

Logan sat at his desk, fit to be tied. He decided to get started on clearing out his things. With one angry yank, he pulled out a drawer, and sent it and its contents splattering to the floor. Logan sighed. He looked up.

Kelly was standing there.

Her presence shocked him. The first thing he could think of was the evidence of his own carelessness lying on the floor. He looked at her as if to say, Oh yeah? I meant that! Then to prove it, he furiously started dumping all the other drawers, as well. He left them all in a pile on the floor near his feet. Then he looked up again, mortified.

"What?" he cried, angrily.

The tone of his voice made Kelly back off a bit. Then when it seemed safer, she advanced, cautiously.

She looked upset, but more hurt and bewildered than angry. Logan was too embarrassed to look her in the eye. He had not meant to do her any harm. She should have known better than to get involved with divorced men susceptible to young blondes. The soft tone of her voice and her quizzical words made him feel even worse.

"What . . . happened?" she said.

Logan could not keep civil. "I haven't got time to discuss it right now. There's an excellent account available in the *Post*. A bit lurid, but very provocative reading."

Just leave me alone, he thought. Take your wonded look and your compassionate queries somewhere else.

"I read the *Post*," she said, quietly.

Logan went back to dumping files, just to look down. "So you already know. Or you think you know . . ."

Kelly was pleading now. "Tell me otherwise. Tell me you didn't sleep with my client."

Logan would not respond. He did not wish to lie to her, so what could he have said? He wanted to tell her the truth, her above all; but he knew that that was impossible. He just kept stacking files.

"Dammit, Logan," she said, with exasperation.

Logan looked up, quickly. "Dammit, Logan? Is that what you just said? I bust my ass helping you out, wind up losing my job— I'm held up to public ridicule, the number one joke in a city of ten million people, and you said—dammit, Logan!"

"Dammit, Logan, you didn't have to sleep with her!"

This was underneath it all, he knew; they could keep talking about my client and your case, crimes and conduct, and all they were really talking about were affection and jealousy. And all at the top of their lungs.

"You're right!" he screamed. "You're absolutely right! Mea culpa, my mistake. I should have thrown her out the door—well, I'm paying for it. Me. No one else. Tom Logan. Ex-Assistant District Attorney."

Kelly put her hands on her hips. "Stop flattering yourself. *I'm* paying for it, too—Chelsea most of all. She was in enough trouble as it was—you didn't have to turn her into a public whore."

Logan was about to respond with a base remark—something about her being one to begin with—but he held back. He hadn't thought much about Chelsea sitting in a jail cell, confused, helpless and lonely. He had been concentrating on her probable lies and her complete irresponsibility. The conflicting images upset him now. He could only sigh and turn away.

"Jesus . . ." he said. "Just get out of here."

Logan took a swipe at his desk now. He threw the papers that lay atop it flying to the floor.

Looking down, he did not see the expression forming on Kelly's face. It was, despite all she was suffering, sympathetic. She hesitated, now knowing how to help. Then she shrugged.

She yanked out a file of her own and dumped it on the floor.

Logan stopped. He looked down with disbelief at the new papers and articles now littering his office. Then he looked back up at Kelly. She was smiling and nodding, with satisfaction.

"What was that?" he asked.

"What was what?"

"What you just did there."

"I was helping you."

"Well, don't. Don't ever help me with anything ever again!"

Logan shook his head. He went back to his own dumping. Imagine that, he thought, Kelly horning in on my desecration. Who did she think she was?

"Oh," he said, as an afterthought. "Good luck with your trial. I'm behind you all the way."

Kelly made a face. "Tom Logan, my biggest fan."

"You bet I am. If you don't clear Chelsea, I don't stand a chance in hell of getting my job back. And that's all I want right now—the life I had the day before I met you."

Kelly braved the remarks. She appreciated him wishing her good luck, no matter how selfishly motivated it was. And she knew the selfishness was just a front. She thought for a minute, watching the desperate man trash his office.

"If we're both all finished up with the personal abuse here," she said, "I've got . . . sort of an idea."

Logan did not look up. She continued, in a louder voice.

"Since you and I each have such a vital stake in clearing Chelsea—granted, for different reasons . . ."

"Stop," Logan said, quickly. "Don't even think about it. Not now. Never."

Kelly sighed; he was so smart. "Just for one case. Personal considerations aside, up to now we've had an extremely positive working relationship."

"Work with *you* again? Me?"

"Is that a 'yes' or a 'no'?"

"That's a no."

Come on, tough guy, she thought, give it up. Logan turned his back on her, shuffling and chucking away papers.

"Pooling our considerable legal talents," she pressed, "there isn't the slightest doubt in my mind Chelsea will be acquitted."

Logan stopped. He had to admit this was true, and it sounded tempting. "No," he said, to agree.

"You'll get your job back and I'll be on my way . . ."

She could tell by his silence that he was seriously considering it. And as ever, of course, she was right.

"No way," Logan kept saying. "No way."

Chapter Nineteen

There was no way it was going to work.

Logan and Kelly, together, in a tiny East Village office? Logan had no doubts both of them were making a big mistake.

The place was about the size of three telephone booths. Most of it was taken up by Kelly's desk; the remaining space held a filing cabinet, two chairs, and one answering machine. Kelly, however, had also found room for several bizarre pieces of art—some looked like crumpled paper, some like human organs, some were simply indescribable. They were, she informed him, payments she had received in lieu of money.

"I knew it," he told her. "This won't work."

"I'm only slightly less unhappy than you are about it, Logan," she answered. "But the least we can do is give it a try."

Kelly's idea of "trying" was simple: she stretched a piece of masking tape down the center of the desk. Then she jammed two chairs together behind it.

"You get one side," she explained. "I get the other. You have three drawers on your side, I have three drawers on my side. We'll share the center drawer. The phone goes right in the middle."

Logan sighed. He looked at the arrangement; then he looked around the entire miniscule office. Already he missed the world of prosecution.

He had no choice but to try and get used to it. Hesitantly, he sat in the chair on the right side. Kelly sat down in the chair on the left. The sides of their legs were touching but neither considered it amorously; they just felt cramped.

Logan looked at a particularly bizarre piece of art that was placed on the desk. Pointedly, he transferred it over to Kelly's side. She sighed and nodded. There was a pause as the two passengers— definitely in economy class—pondered their upcoming journey.

"I'm messy," Logan said then.

"I'm not," Kelly answered.

"My side of the desk will tend to get very, very messy. I like it that way. Don't ever straighten up anything for me."

No problem, Kelly thought. "Promise."

Sitting there, the quarters began to seem especially tight. Their legs darted in and out from under the desk in fruitless searches for comfort. Their legs constantly touched doing it and each pulled away when it happened. It was beginning to feel more than just cramped.

"Let's talk about Chelsea's defense," Kelly said, decisively.

Logan jumped. Kelly's foot was accidentally finding its way up his leg. She immediately withdrew it, embarrassed.

"In my opinion," Kelly said, trying to sound businesslike, "we have to cloud the issues in this trial. Get the focus off Chelsea. The two witnesses . . . can we discredit them? Do they have criminal records? Do they pay their bills? What do their neighbors think of them? Parking tickets, bounced checks . . ."

Logan looked at her, dismayed. He shook his head. "Any trick in the book—anything to get the client off."

"Logan, you're a *defense attorney* now. You're *supposed* to get the client off."

Logan blushed a bit. Oh, yeah, he thought.

"We need more room," he said, quickly. "I can't pace. I'm a pacer . . ."

Logan immediately rose. He walked to the few steps to the door and pulled it open. Then he went out into the hall, searching for pacing space.

Kelly continued the conversation; all she saw were fleeting glimpses of Logan, pacing in and out of the doorway. His voice came and went, as well.

"Let's start with the basics," he said. "Is she guilty? Do you think she killed Taft?"

"I think she's capable of killing someone."

"Well, I don't think she killed Taft. The whole case is based on circumstantial evidence."

"Absolutely. That means we don't have to disprove anything— we just have to cast doubt on it."

There was silence for awhile. She saw flashes of blonde hair and suit going by and going away. Kelly screwed up her courage then.

"There's one more important issue involved," she said, gingerly. "Are you . . . going to sleep with our client again?"

Logan passed out of sight. She heard him stop. She didn't hear him say anything for a minute.

"What does that have to do with this trial?" he said, finally.

"It has everything to do with our working relationship." She probed, delicately. "After all, she's an attractive young girl . . ."

"Extremely," Logan's voice said.

"I didn't say extremely attractive, I just said attractive."

There was a pause.

"Extremely," Logan said again.

"She's . . . got a nice body . . ."

"A sensational body."

Kelly sighed. "Will you let me pick the adjectives? A nice body . . . Big eyes . . ."

"Hypnotic eyes. Unforgettable eyes."

Kelly was beside herself. She stood up at her desk. "Dammit, are you going to sleep with her again or not?"

Logan appeared in the doorway then. His smile told her he had only been kidding.

"No," he said.

Kelly collected herself. She cleared her throat and regained a professional demeanor. "Well—good. That's all I wanted to know." She sat down, primly, again. "Now—can we get to work on something important?"

Logan walked slowly back into their office. He sat down beside Kelly again. He could not help noticing how pleased his learned colleague looked. Their legs touched beneath the desk.

Chapter Twenty

The arraignment the next day was standing room only.

This was no normal case and not a mere sensational one; this case had hit the front pages of everything from *The Midnight Globe* to *The Wall Street Journal*. The stands were packed with journalists from all the media and with hordes of thrillseekers, as well. This case had everything: murder, sex, political corruption. This case was entertainment.

Logan and Kelly watched as the prosecution entered. It was Blanchard, of course, looking pleased as punch for an opportunity to make his name—and smear his old rival's. He even flashed a nasty little smile to them as he took his seat. Logan returned one just as mean.

Then Chelsea entered.

She was dressed soberly, in muted colors. Her blonde hair had been carefully brushed. She looked drained and a bit weak; but she still retained the odd mix of defiance and skittishness that had caught Logan's eye in the first place. It was catching the eyes of everyone in the room.

A woman police officer led her slowly to the defense table. As Chelsea approached, her eyes suddenly met Logan's. Seeing him, they filled with both fear and relief.

She reached out to take his hand—not to shake it, but to grasp it for affection and strength. Logan turned the touch into a firm, hearty, innocent hand shake. Standing next to him, Kelly nodded with approval.

Logan spoke to Chelsea quietly and calmly, with no signs of any personal involvement.

"Soon there'll be a jury over there, watching your every move," he said. "You must control your emotions, understand?"

Chelsea gave no sign of disappointment. Apparently it was enough for her just to be near him again—even if it was at her own trial. She withdrew her hand from Logan's, obediently. Then with decorum, she seated herself at the defense table.

"All rise," the clerk said.

Judge Dawkins entered. He was a stout, middle-aged man whom Logan had always considered fair. To the prosecution, that is. He began to sweat a little.

The clerk continued. "Supreme Court for the County and State of New York is now in session. Draw near and ye shall be heard. Honorable Judge John Dawkins presiding."

Dawkins took his place at the bench. He gave a small nod to the clerk.

"Please be seated," he announced. "Your Honor, the case for the People of the State of New York versus Chelsea Elizabeth Deardon is ready to proceed for arraignment. Counsel is present and defendant is present."

"With respect to this matter of change of venue," Dawkins said, "does Defense wish to engage in oral argument?"

Logan rose. "No, Your Honor."

Kelly rose then, too. "Yes."

Logan looked at his partner; he thought they had ironed all of this out during their preparation. His smile was deadly.

"We don't, Your Honor," he said, pointedly.

"Of course we do," Kelly said.

There was a pause during which all in the courtroom could hear Judge Dawkins unhappily sigh.

"Which is it?" he asked.

Kelly jumped in. "We move for a change of venue, due to unreasonable and misleading exposure in the press."

Logan was livid. "I object!"

There was another pause before Dawkins spoke some more bewildered words.

"You object to your own co-counsel's motion?" he asked.

"I do," Logan answered.

Dawkins sighed again. "Would Defense counsel please approach the bench for a moment?"

Logan looked with true annoyance at Kelly as they made their way up; Kelly looked back at him with obstinate righteousness. The courtroom around them buzzed.

When they arrived, Dawkins covered his microphone with a hand. Then with ebbing patience, he leaned slowly forward.

"Boys and girls," he said, "is this the way things are going to go?"

"Your Honor," Kelly answered, "everybody in New York has read about this case . . ."

Logan was incredulous. "So you want to move the trial to a place where people's moral judgments are *looser* than those of New Yorkers?"

"I happen to be talking to His Honor, Mr. Logan," Kelly said, prissily.

Just then, another voice interrupted them; a voice coming from behind them. Blanchard's.

"Would defense counsel please make up its mind," he said, "as to who's going to be its spokesperson? Otherwise, this could be the longest arraignment in the history of jurisprudence."

Dawkins looked at Logan and Kelly with an expression that said that Blanchard had a point. Then he pointed them both back to the defense table.

Logan and Kelly were still arguing quietly as they walked back. But Dawkins' pronouncement silenced them.

"Motion denied."

Logan nodded, as if to say, See? Kelly shrugged back. There was nothing more she could do; the Mighty Oz had spoken.

"Does Defense wish to enter a plea?" Judge Dawkins asked.

"We do," Kelly answered. "Chelsea Elizabeth Deardon pleads— not guilty."

"The Court will note for the record your plea of not guilty." The Judge nodded again at the clerk. "Call the next case."

Kelly and Logan looked at each other. They were shaken but not unprepared.

"Just a minute, Your Honor," Kelly said. "We'd like to make a motion for bail."

Blanchard was on it, immediately. "The People object to setting any bail and ask that the defendant be remanded to custody with no bail pending trial. Had the defendant not been apprehended on the morning after the murder, she would still be a fugitive and at large."

"Your Honor," Logan said now, "under New York state law, a fugitive from justice can be detained by any official of the judiciary system."

"The fugitive laws don't pertain here!" Blanchard shot back. "The defendant was arrested by the police."

Logan and Kelly again exchanged glances. The look meant they would have to use a last resort plan, one that it would be better for Kelly to introduce.

"Wrong!" Kelly replied. "Willingly, and by her own initiative, Chelsea Deardon turned herself into Tom Logan's custody hours before the police arrived. Why else would she go immediately from the scene of the crime to the apartment of an assistant district attorney?"

Blanchard's eyes widened, amazed at this tactic.

"And immediately into his bed!" he shouted.

The crowd had been waiting for something like this. Immediately, gasps, laughter and excited murmuring went through it. For the moment, the courtroom seemed like a theater in which a highly provocative play was being performed.

Logan had expected this, too, of course. Still, he could not help feeling mortified at having his personal business so publicly aired and by a nincompoop such as Blanchard. He looked at him, as if to say, You should be so lucky, pal.

Judge Dawkins banged his gavel, furiously.

"Order!" he cried. Then he directed his wrath at Blanchard. "Counsel, any more outbursts like that and I'll hold you in contempt. I've heard enough and I'm prepared to rule now. Bail is set for fifty thousand dollars! This court is adjourned!"

The new defense team looked at each other with satisfaction. Then they beamed two very satisfied smiles at the fuming, blushing Blanchard.

Kelly signed Chelsea out. The young defendant sat patiently in the prison office as Kelly performed the transaction and obtained the release papers.

She looked at Kelly with an expression of bottomless gratitude. Combined with her constant other-worldly look it gave Chelsea an angelic appearance. Why would any man want a woman like this? Kelly wondered. You'd have to always be taking care of her. She sighed, figuring there would never be any explaining.

Once the papers were signed, Chelsea moved forward, intending to embrace Kelly in thanks. Embarrassed, Kelly shoved the release papers towards her for her signature and managed to avoid it.

The two women walked slowly out onto the jailhouse steps, into a sunny day. Kelly winced and hid her eyes. Chelsea directed her face up to the sky, seeming to bathe in the warmth and brightness.

"Once you get past the grotesque fascination," she remarked, "jail sucks."

Kelly nodded. "We got you out as quickly as we could."

There was a discernible tone of impatience in Kelly's voice; she seemed now to deal with Chelsea only dutifully and Chelsea noticed.

"Look," she said, directly, "I did not kill Victor Taft."

Kelly did not address the issue. She spoke almost in warning, "Well, it's going to take a lot of work to convince a jury of that. So . . . no more secrets, no more imaginary diaries, no more half-truths—got it?"

Chelsea nodded, chastened. Then she looked away from Kelly, as if more for sympathetic counsel. Kelly noticed her wandering, questioning gaze and sighed.

"He's at the office—planning your defense," she explained.

"I was . . . sort of hoping he'd be here," Chelsea admitted.

Kelly chose her words carefully now. She wanted to speak as professionally as she could and not let jealousy or anger color her comments. It wasn't going to be easy.

"Chelsea," she said, "you'd better play it straight with us. You cost Tom Logan his job, and in return for it he's helping you."

Chelsea immediately seemed miserable and intensely sorry. She looked at Kelly, as if searching for anything, anything she could do for him in return. Kelly tried to ignore this, too. It was even harder.

Kelly immediately took Chelsea's hand and led her down the stairs to the street. She was just like a child, Kelly thought. Men were just nuts.

Chapter Twenty-One

Logan for the Defense worked even harder than Logan for the People. He dedicated himself all day and night to Chelsea's case, using every waking moment—and for him, that meant plenty—to clearing her. He knew she would not be the only one on the stand. He would be on trial, as well.

Kelly kept up his pace. The two of them questioned any possible witnesses around Taft's apartment house; they took countless depositions; they spent entire days in the library and in the Hall of Records. They grilled Chelsea mercilessly in endless courtroom simulations—with Logan, of course, credibly playing the D.A. They hardly had time to eat more than hot dogs from sidewalk stands, which heartily offended Kelly's palate. This time, however, she did not mind. The company made it all worthwhile.

She even learned to defer to Logan on certain issues and he to her on others. She let him question Cavanaugh himself, for instance, and only interrupted a few times. Soon they did not quarrel at all over expertise, procedure or rank. They were in the best—and most platonic—sense of the word, married.

Logan even had to combine his days with Jennifer with work. Jennifer enjoyed every minute of it. She loved to see her father gainfully employed, utilizing his considerable mental abilities. And she loved to see how he and Kelly worked so well side-by-side. She was beginning to like the feisty but kind young lawyer a lot. She remembered how her father had described her as "really terrific." She was better than that crazy lady with the wet hair any day.

One night, Logan had gone out to shop for dinner, leaving Jennifer and Kelly alone. Kelly was reading through yet another stack of legal documents. She looked truly exhausted. Jennifer decided to give her a break.

She sneaked up behind her and started massaging her tense, weary shoulders. Kelly moaned in surprise and gratitude.

"Dad always likes this, too," Jennifer said, unsubtly. "You guys have a lot in common."

"Yeah," Kelly said, "aching shoulders and a shaky defense of Chelsea Deardon."

"More than that. I mean, you like each other, don't you?"

"He has his good points."

"I've seen the way you guys look at each other."

Was it that obvious? Kelly grew slightly defensive now. "Well, I like the way he moves . . ."

"Yeah, until he trips over something."

Kelly looked at Jennifer and the two of them laughed. Suddenly, she felt allied to this kid, even if she was a bit of a maneuverer.

Then they heard the door open.

Logan came in. He was carrying two bags of groceries. He stopped and smiled a minute at the two of them.

"Any calls?" he said.

"Just Mom," Jennifer answered. "She's on her way over."

Logan nodded and proceeded into the kitchen with the bags. When he was out of sight, Kelly glanced at Jennifer, knowingly. There was a second of silence. Then they heard one of the bags fall heavily to the floor. Jennifer and Kelly both cracked up.

Both of them headed into the kitchen then. There they saw the man of the apartment standing helplessly before a mess of broken eggs and jelly. Sighing, Kelly brought over a broom and Jennifer a dustpan.

As they cleaned, Kelly looked leadingly at Jennifer. Then she cleared her throat. Finally, Logan's daughter got the hint.

"Dad," she said, "Mom and I had a long talk."

"Oh?" Logan said.

"Yes. And . . . I got her to cancel the subpoena."

There was a pause. Logan just looked, astonished, at Jennifer. "How did you do *that?*"

Jennifer took a deep breath. She looked briefly at Kelly then back at her father. Then she answered.

"I told her it would be all right with you if I went to California."

There was an even longer pause. Jennifer dropped the last piece of broken eggshell in the trash. Logan just followed her with his eyes. At last, he was able to respond.

"What?"

"But in return," Jennifer said, quickly, "you get to pick me up in L.A. on June first and keep me for sixty consecutive days."

Kelly corrected her, under her breath. "Ninety."

"Right," Jennifer said. "Ninety consecutive days."

Logan turned slowly to face Jennifer's vocal coach. "How do *you* know, Kelly?"

"Who, me?" Kelly played dumb.

"You did this," he said, sharply. "You really thought I'd buy a deal like that?"

Now that her cover was blown, Kelly began to whole-heartedly state her case. "Look, Logan, right now you get her four days a month—forty-eight days a year. We got you an extra thirty-two days."

"That's almost double," Jennifer chimed in.

"I can add," Logan said, flatly.

Suddenly, a car horn interrupted their debate. Logan looked at his daughter, pained. He hated to see her go even today—how would he feel with her completely across the country?

Still, he had to admit, Kelly had done a pretty good deal for him. He hadn't exactly qualified for Father of the Year with this Chelsea business. And if it *was* almost double the amount of days . . .

"There's Mom," Jennifer said. She turned, hopefully, to Logan. "What do I tell her?"

Logan did not answer for a minute. Then he figured it was indeed the best compromise possible, even if it *was* Beverly Hills.

"Tell her it's a deal," he said.

Jennifer nearly hooted. She went into Logan's arms and gave him a great hug. Then from his embrace, she looked over at Kelly.

"What a team you guys are," she said. "You really have a lot in common."

As if not wanting to face the consequences of her latest nudge, Jennifer fled from the kitchen and the apartment. On her way out, she gave Kelly one last, affectionate, secretive wink.

There was a patch of silence after she was gone. Kelly took the time just to look at Logan, warmly. Logan tried to evade her eyes.

"What did she mean," he asked, evasively, "we have a lot in common?"

"She thinks you like me," Kelly said, simply.

The words were at last out in the open. They seemed suddenly to change things between them, to reduce their distance from each other, even in actual space. Just then, they seemed to be nose to nose, mouth to mouth, eye to eye. Indeed, their eyes had locked; they seemed entranced.

Logan could not look away from Kelly. The days and nights he had spent with her, the meals, the laughs, the findings they had shared—all of them had made him dependent on Kelly, and not just as a lawyer. He had never felt as close to her as he did at that moment—or been as close. His words were still evasive, but he uttered them in a dreamy, far-off sort of way.

"She's only a kid," he said, "what does she know?"

"She's a very bright kid," Kelly replied.

Logan could not stop himself then. He moved even closer to Kelly. She moved even closer to him. They were too close for talking now. They were too close for anything but kissing.

Kiss they did, a long, warm and deep kiss. It felt strange and scary and exciting to kiss after so many weeks as colleagues, adversaries, partners. It felt for both of them incredibly, unprecedentedly intimate.

They did not kiss for long. After maybe a minute, they pulled apart at the same exact time. Neither knew how far they could or should go that night. At any rate, they had already taken the first crucial step.

"I . . . better hit the road . . ." Kelly said, panting a little.

"Big day tomorrow," Logan sighed.

She moved away from him in slow motion, drifted to the door. Logan kept watching her, smiling, softly. She pulled the door open, tentatively, as if not sure she would really be exiting through it. Logan waited, with as much unsurety.

But neither one moved towards the other. They kept the same, agitated distance.

"Well . . . night . . ." Kelly said.

"See you in the morning," Logan said.

She was gone then.

Logan just stood there, smiling. Life was full of surprises, he thought. If only it were full of women like Laura Kelly.

Immediately, he had an idea. He headed at full speed towards the front hall closet. That was where his umbrella was.

Gotta dance, he thought.

Chapter Twenty-Two

A suspect could do worse than have people in love as her lawyers. That crossed Logan's mind as he awaited the trial's start the next morning.

Already he felt raring to go. He had Chelsea to clear; he had his own reputation to save. And now he had a new reason to excel: Laura. He wished to do well for her and with her. It was their first case together, that was the point; let other people have dates, he thought, these were lawyers here. The best lawyers. They were going to cut Blanchard to pieces.

The prosecution was already ponderously presenting his case. He paced, he glared, he chuckled, ominously. Above all, he avoided Logan and Kelly's alert and confident faces as he made his opening statements.

"Ladies and gentlemen, we, the People, are prepared to prove beyond a reasonable doubt that on the night of October seventh, Chelsea Elizabeth Deardon did commit the crime of murder against the person of one Victor Taft, that with intent to cause the death of Victor Taft she shot him in the chest three times."

As Blanchard droned on, Logan's attention wandered to the crowd of fascinated spectators. Among them, he spied a very nervous Maxwell Bower. Behind him, Logan saw a very cool Robert Forrester. He slowly addressed his attention again to Blanchard.

"We will call witnesses who will testify under oath that they saw Chelsea Deardon flee the scene of the crime. Ballistics will prove that the gun used to kill Victor Taft was registered in the name of Chelsea Deardon."

Logan checked Laura out. She seemed just as calm and confident as *he* was. He was glad to see it. He smiled at her; she smiled back.

"In other words," Blanchard continued, "we will prove that Chelsea Deardon was *at* the scene of the crime, possessed the means to *commit* the crime and had every opportunity to do so."

Now Blanchard turned his back to the jury. He spoke the end of his statement to Logan and Kelly.

"Opportunity and means. Crucial evidence which, by themselves, are enough to establish guilt beyond a reasonable doubt in a murder case. But we will also provide a compelling *motive*."

Slowly, Logan turned again to Kelly. She wore the same curious expression as he did. Motive? What was Blanchard pulling?

"This was a crime," he said, "committed by a woman who was secretly Victor Taft's lover for two years, during which time he was her only means of financial support."

Logan looked over at Chelsea. She was staring ahead, impassively.

"Is this true?" he asked, stunned.

She kept staring; she did not respond. Yet her bottom lip perceptibly trembled.

"Explicit love letters found in the safe deposit box of the deceased will prove that the love affair between Chelsea Deardon and Victor Taft was volatile and even violent on occasion."

Both Logan and Kelly now stared with angry disbelief at their client. Chelsea did not meet their eyes.

"We will prove," Blanchard continued, "that Victor Taft finally ended this stormy relationship leaving Chelsea Deardon on her own, without support and seeking revenge. We will prove that, in her frustration and rage, she murdered Victor Taft in cold blood. In response to such a brutal crime, the People have no alternative but to demand that you return the maximum sentence allowed in the State of New York—life imprisonment, with no possibility of parole. Thank you."

Now Chelsea looked down at the table, concealing her eyes from her lawyers. Logan continued to stare at her, crushed. Then he looked at Kelly. She was equally decimated.

Chelsea was full of surprises, Logan thought. Even when her life depended on it. Logan grew furious, thinking of how he had risked his career and even the custody of his daughter for her. What kind of woman *was* this?

He stood, trying to conceal his rage.

"Your Honor," he said, "we request a brief recess before opening remarks."

Judge Dawkins nodded.

"Granted." He pounded his gavel. "This court will be recessed for fifteen minutes."

In the conference room, it took a few minutes for Logan to say anything. He paced the floor, carefully weighing his words. Should he be cagey, subtle? Should he use psychology? Or should he just let her have it with both barrels?

Logan opted for the latter.

"It's been one lie after another, hasn't it?" he yelled at Chelsea. "We looked like incompetent idiots in there!"

Chelsea seemed ready to fall to pieces. Yet her fragility did not impress either of her lawyers, not that day. They had seen that pose once too often.

"Why didn't you tell us about your relationship?" Kelly said then. "Did you really think you could keep a lid on that?"

Chelsea swallowed, slowly. When she replied, she spoke only to Kelly; she could not bring herself to address Logan on this issue.

"I was hoping," she said, faintly, "I mean, it wasn't common knowledge. Victor and I never went out in public together. I thought if you knew, it would only make me look more guilty."

Logan shook his head. He was ready to give this up right now. In fact, he wished he were on the prosecution side; he would nail Chelsea in about twenty seconds flat.

"You went to Taft's apartment," he said. "You had a fight and you killed him."

Chelsea hid her face in her hands. "No—no, I didn't. We had a fight but I didn't kill him."

It was Kelly's turn to be hard on her now.

"You shot Taft and then you went to Logan's to get him emotionally involved so he would clear everything."

Chelsea was shaking uncontrollably. "I went to Logan's because I was scared. Why don't you believe me? I didn't kill anyone!"

Chelsea began to cry then, great, child-like tears. Kelly remained unmoved. She just looked skeptically at Logan. Then she spoke as if Chelsea weren't even in the room.

"That's the most preposterous explanation I've ever heard," Kelly said.

Logan looked down at Chelsea. He was not exactly touched by the sight of her, but he was a little swayed. He thought she was an unstable girl, an impulsive girl, an untrustworthy girl—but he did not think she was a violent girl. It just didn't fit.

"Yes, it is," he said, "but I believe her."

Kelly looked at him, stupefied. "Based on what—her track record so far?"

"Call it a hunch. Instinct."

"I hope it's coming from above the waist."

Logan shot her a look that said, That's unfair. Kelly smiled, apologetically, agreeing. Then she checked her watch. There was

136

no time for a long debate. She was just going to have to trust Logan's experience.

"Okay," she said, reluctantly, "I believe her, too, she's telling us the truth. But it's going to take some fancy footwork in there."

Logan grinned, slowly. She had come to the right place.

Chapter Twenty-Three

Logan knew he would have to think of something fast.

His mind was racing all the way back to the courtroom. He knew they were operating at a disadvantage from the word go. The jury already knew he and Kelly had been caught by surprise; they had even had to call a recess. All this made them look unprepared; it also made them look gullible. How could a jury believe in Chelsea if her own lawyers couldn't even trust her?

He knew he was going to have to transfer all his prosecutorial guile to the defense table now. He searched his memory for all his own best tricks, his most surprising tactics. But it was all in reverse; with so little time, it was confusing to have to turn it around. It was like trying to tie somebody else's shoes. He remembered how it had been with Jennifer as a kid. He would have to do better than *that*.

When he stood before the jury to give his opening statement, he paced for a longer time than usual. He could think of nothing; it was as if he were an imposter in the courtroom, as if he had not even gone to law school. Finally, when he seemed to have been pacing forever—and *that* could only look like he had no ideas—he decided to begin. Any which way he could.

"Ladies and gentlemen," he said, "we contend that Chelsea Deardon had no motive to kill Victor Taft. The defense has presented a version of a *possible* motive, but it's all based on conjecture, hearsay and . . ."

He could hear the insincerity in his voice; how could the jury not? If he were on it, he wouldn't believe himself. Many of them weren't even looking at him; they were busy glaring at Chelsea, trying to imagine her the star of the whole lurid story the prosecution had told them. They could be titillated and then condemn the star of their fantasy; they could enjoy themselves *and* absolve themselves; it was perfect. How could a wavering, incoherent defense attorney compete?

Logan shot a look at Kelly. He feared she would be looking at him, crestfallen, all her hopes in him dashed. Instead she seemed calm, trusting in him. That kind of faith gave Logan courage. He stopped suddenly in mid-sentence. Then he turned back to the jury.

"Ladies and gentlemen of the jury, you're not buying anything of this, are you?"

To a man, the jury sat up straight. Every distracted face came his way; every roving eye focused on him. And it all seemed, Logan thought with relief, as if that had been his plan all along.

"I didn't think so," he continued. "Well, to tell you the truth, after listening to Mr. Blanchard lay out the prosecution's evidence, even *I'm* convinced my client murdered Victor Taft."

Now not only was the jury riveted to Logan, everybody else in the courtroom was. Blanchard stared at him in shock; Judge Dawkins studied him, intrigued; even Kelly sat forward, hanging on his every word. Great, he thought, now *you* tell me what to say next.

"After all," he went on, "if *I* had walked into that room and found Victor Taft dead on the floor and Chelsea Deardon's fingerprints on the weapon that killed him, there isn't a thing in the world that could convince me she wasn't guilty. I don't think a reasonable mind could come to any other conclusion."

Logan saw Blanchard turn, with a worried expression, to his assistant. Soon the prosecutor was whispering in his ear.

"What the hell is he up to . . ."

Wouldn't *you* like to know, Logan thought, triumphantly. Wouldn't *I* like to know!

"Let's save a little time here," the defense attorney went on. "We've all got other things we'd rather be doing. Now just be honest. Is there anybody here who doesn't believe Chelsea Deardon is guilty?"

A mixture of laughter and surprise went up from the audience. Blanchard wasn't whispering then; he was on his feet, shouting.

"Objection, Your Honor!"

Logan thanked Blanchard privately for his perfect entrance; every great performer needs a foil, he thought. Logan played straight man, steamrolling over Blanchard's remarks.

"Come on," he told the jury, "don't hold back! Look, *my* hand is up! I'm convinced she murdered Victor Taft in cold blood! Isn't everybody convinced?"

Holding his hand up, ingenuously, Logan looked down the length of the jury. Then still standing that way, he turned, quizzically, to Kelly.

"*You're* convinced, aren't you?"

Kelly looked at him with bemused awe. Then she nodded; she was if he was.

Soon Logan and Kelly were not the only ones holding their hands up. Like an obedient class, the jury started slowly raising their hands. One by one, they began visibly and silently attesting to the guilt of the woman they had come to judge. Impartially.

Blanchard stepped farther forward, clearly beside himself.

"Your Honor . . ." he began to protest.

140

"There you have it, Your Honor!" Logan cried over him. "The prosecution thinks she's guilty and the Assistant D.A. wouldn't represent facts wrongly, would he? Everybody on the jury thinks she's guilty. Well, shouldn't we save the state of New York a lot of time and money by moving directly to sentencing?"

This was too much for Judge Dawkins. He went very quickly from being intrigued to being offended. He banged his gavel loudly.

"Mr. Logan!" he exploded. "You are totally out of order and you know it! This jury is disqualified. Court will be recessed while I consider citing defense counsel for contempt."

Logan stopped, panting a little. He was even a bit surprised at himself. Yet somewhere, somehow, he actually felt he had come up with a coherent—if outlandish—opening statement. He did not want to have to stop it in mid-stream.

"Your Honor," he said, quietly, "with all due respect, this jury may believe my client is guilty at this time, but I state for the record that I believe in this jury and I'm willing to continue and accept their final verdict."

Nonplussed, cooling down, Dawkins considered Logan's comments. As if he could not believe he was doing this, he turned for confirmation to Kelly. Kelly nodded, encouragingly, at him.

"I concur, Your Honor," she said.

Finally, the judge looked over at Blanchard. The attorney for the People smiled, wearily.

"The prosecution has equal faith in this jury, Your Honor."

Dawkins sighed, heavily. Then he pounded his gavel one more time. "Very well. Proceed, Mr. Logan."

Logan smiled, gratefully. As if he had never been interrupted, he turned quickly to the jury. Behind him, Blanchard sheepishly regained his seat.

"Thank you, Your Honor," Logan said. "So. If we all think she's guilty, what should we do?"

This question, of course, was rhetorical. But an old woman on the jury was obviously caught up in the dilemma and answered, audibly.

"Surely she's entitled to a fair trial."

There were some titters from the audience. Judge Dawkins scowled at the woman, who smiled back, weakly, realizing her error. Logan smiled kindly at her, appreciating her interest.

"Ah," he said, "so you do want to give her a fair trial before we convict her. It's quite a problem, isn't it?"

Slowly, Logan walked over to the court blackboard. He picked up the chalk and slowly, deliberately, he wrote three words upon it.

"PRESUMPTION OF INNOCENCE."

Then he turned back and faced the jury again.

"Everybody sure what that means?" He waited, just in case the old woman was game again. "It means that whatever assumptions you might already have about this case, Chelsea Deardon must be seen in your eyes, believed in your minds, understood in your *hearts*, to be innocent. The law requires that of you."

Out of the corner of his eye, Logan could see Blanchard sighing, in disgust. He was well aware that, far from putting the jury off, Logan had won them over to his side.

"The burden of proof," Logan said, "is totally on the prosecution, as Mr. Blanchard well knows. Chelsea Deardon isn't even required to defend herself."

Logan waited until he was sure the jury had comprehended those words. He checked the audience to see if they had, as well. Sitting among them he happened to spy Robert Forrester. He slowly turned back.

"Chelsea Deardon sits before you today as a completely innocent woman. Burn that into your minds."

He thought they might check out Chelsea at this point, but all eyes stayed fixed on him. All right! Logan thought.

"I'll admit that Mr. Blanchard has skillfully pieced together an overwhelming amount of circumstantial evidence, but no matter how damaging it may seem to my client right now, that's all it is—circumstantial—and incorrect."

Logan glanced over casually to the defense table. Kelly was giving him a subtle "thumbs-up" sign. Logan looked past her and back to the audience, back to Robert Forrester.

Logan caught his eyes. Forrester quickly glanced away.

"So what is the truth?" Logan went on. "Well, maybe the truth begins eighteen years ago, when dozens of paintings by the defendant's father, Sebastian Deardon, supposedly perished in a fire which tragically took his life. The insurance paid on those paintings totalled two and a half million dollars. A staggering sum but only a fraction of what they're worth today; for we claim those paintings still exist and are now worth more than twenty million dollars."

Both the jury and the audience audibly agreed: it was a lot of money.

"This is a complex case, ladies and gentlemen. A road filled with twists and turns. But I'm confident that all of us, working together, will finally arrive at the truth. And the truth is that Victor Taft wasn't murdered out of passion by the defendant. Victor Taft was murdered to protect someone. Someone who, seventeen years ago, was himself a conspirator to arson, fraud and murder. Someone who took advantage of Chelsea Deardon and framed her for the crime for which he himself is responsible."

That was it, Logan thought, leave them hanging. He did not smile at the jury; he merely solemnly nodded. Then he walked slowly over to the defense table and sat down.

Dawkins banged his gavel.

"With no objections, court is adjourned until nine o'clock, Monday morning."

The courtroom exploded then with loud chatter and conjecture. All the talk, of course, was focused on the audacious defense attorney. Blanchard was hardly on anyone's lips or mind.

Kelly turned to Logan. Her eyes were filled with grateful tears, yet she was smiling. She didn't say a word but the way she touched Logan's arm was statement enough.

The two of them rose. Chelsea joined them. She, too, was silent but she looked at Logan with some emotion beyond love, desire or respect; it was closer to worship.

The three of them started up the aisle. The courtroom was swiftly emptying, but one man had conspicuously and purposely stayed behind.

Robert Forrester.

He started angrily down the aisle. He did not stop until he was face to face with Logan.

"Look," he said, "I won't be made a scapegoat for the desperate act of an emotionally disturbed woman, is that clear?"

Forrester was hardly his cool, erudite self, Logan thought with some pleasure. There were even drops of some very uncouth sweat on his brow. How gauche.

"If you'll excuse me," Logan said, dismissively.

Forrester placed a surprisingly strong hand on Logan's arm, stopping him. Logan began to shake him off when a sound prevented their scuffle.

It was a word, really, uttered by a female voice. It was spoken without animation but with hard, unshakable certainty.

"Murderer," Chelsea said.

The two men turned toward the blonde woman standing near them. Forrester stared at her with what seemed real disgust.

"What?" he said. "How dare you . . ."

"I was *there*," Chelsea said, with the same conviction.

"A small child was there," Forrester retorted, "hardly qualified to come to a rational conclusion."

Chelsea was staring at him, staring him down. Her look was just as unyielding, just as condemnatory, as her words. Logan had never seen this side to her; he almost felt frightened.

"Your father was an alcoholic," Forrester went on. "He passed out on the floor that night. I tried to save him, but the flames were too intense."

Chelsea was looking through him then. She was looking not at the sophisticate before her, but at her father's studio, her father's painting, her father's flames.

"You're a liar," she said.

The look finally melted Forrester. He had to turn away. Then he had to walk away.

Out in the corridor, Chelsea stood by herself in the corner, recuperating. She stared at the wall, shaking her head, as if trying to dispel her memories.

Logan and Kelly kept their voices to whispers so as not to disturb her. But they could not keep their voices from cracking sometimes with excitement.

"Nice opening, counselor," Kelly said.

Logan shrugged. He had to admit it: once he had warmed up— hell, once he had made it up—it had gone pretty well. There was only one drawback.

"Too bad we can't prove it," he said.

Kelly nodded. "We need to find the Deardon paintings."

"Let's go back to Taft's shipping agent."

In their days of preparation, this had been one of their more frustrating dead ends.

"Trans-Continental Express?" Kelly said. "Legally, they're not compelled to cooperate. They sure didn't give us anything before."

Logan looked at Kelly and grinned. She may have learned something from him today in court; he had learned something from *her* before.

"This time," he said, "we'll use Boston vs. Cavalero."

Chapter Twenty-Four

Actually, it turned out to be a variation of Boston vs. Cavalero. It was a little-known legal precedent in which defense attorneys are allowed to lie their way into fancy offices, provided they have their clients' best interests at heart. And provided that they aren't caught.

It helped if one looked like Tom Logan, who had been known to turn a few women's heads now and then, or so The New York Post claimed. This day, Logan milked his pleasant smile for all it was worth. The receptionist at Trans-Continental Express responded, even if Kelly was there beside him.

"Hi," he said, silkily, "I'm Tom Logan, attorney. I talked to someone about gaining access to some shipping records. Mr. Some-thing . . . in . . . what was it . . . ?"

"Mr. Crane in Records?" she asked, helpfully.

"That's it. Where do I find him?"

The receptionist showed signs of doubt. "Fourteenth floor, but . . ."

Kelly pointed appreciatively at the receptionist then. "Why, isn't

146

that a lovely blouse she's wearing? That's a very lovely blouse you're wearing."

The receptionist smiled, flattered. In the time it took her to check her blouse and look up again, Logan and Kelly were gone.

They were on their way to the fourteenth floor. Once there, they quickly passed by several busy offices. Finally, they found one that was empty. Checking around themselves, cautiously, they entered.

Logan immediately started rummaging through the desk drawers. Kelly immediately picked up the phone.

"Connect me with Crane in Records," she said.

Logan found what he was looking for: a pad of inter-office memos. He rolled one into the typewriter. Then he knocked out a few perfunctory lines.

Kelly got Crane's secretary. "Mr. Crane? Mr. Morrison from Claims is calling. One moment, please."

Kelly pressed the "Hold" button. Then she nodded at Logan. He cleared his throat and picked up.

"Crane?" Logan said. "How many memos do I have to send you people before I get a reply?"

Kelly folded her arms and watched Logan, highly impressed. This guy could have been an actor instead of a lawyer. Maybe they were the same thing. She looked out the door, for any passersby.

"You know what I mean," Logan went on. "For three weeks, I've been requesting the Taft Gallery warehouse shipping file. Customer claims his order never arrived, and my ass is on the line. I need it immediately, *now*, not tomorrow! That's right, Taft. Do I have to spell it for you? Get a copy of the damn thing up to Morrison in claims pronto, or you can face the consequences with the Legal Department!"

Logan slammed the phone down. Then calmly, his anger completely erased, he typed out a few more words. Finally, he pulled

147

the memo out of the typewriter. With the zip of the paper coming out of the carriage, a secretary entered the office.

She stood politely but confusedly before them.

"Yes?" she said. "May I help you?"

Kelly turned, quickly. "Is this the, uh, Claims Department?"

"No, Claims is on the twenty-sixth floor."

Kelly threw up her hands, as if to say Silly me. "I couldn't find water if I fell out of a boat!"

Logan put on an exasperated face; this happened, he suggested, at the Kiwanis Club picnic, too. "Come on, Mildred, Mr. Morrison's waiting."

Swiftly, Logan and Kelly passed by the secretary and fled the office, maintaining a quiet but intense "argument" between themselves. On the way, Logan carefully folded the memo and gave it to Kelly.

Their next stop was the twenty-sixth floor. The Claims Department filled its entire length. Logan and Kelly found themselves searching through many small cubicles with people busily and silently working inside.

At last, they decided to take a chance on a large, imperious secretary who was moving silently down the wall-to-wall carpet towards them.

Logan stopped her with a proud, beaming look.

"Well," he said, "how do I look?"

The woman looked at him, puzzled. Logan chattered on, confidently.

"Joe Morrison. First day on the job. I want to make a good first impression. Which office is mine?"

The woman just kept looking at him. "Morrison? Nobody told me . . . are you sure?"

Sighing, Logan fished for something in his pockets. Then, irritated, he turned to Kelly.

"Mildred," he said, "have you got that memo?"

Kelly smiled, affectionately, at the big lug. "Yes, Mr. Morrison, I've got it right here."

Kelly took the recently folded memo out of her purse and handed it to him. Logan snapped it flat several times. Then he read from it.

" 'Effective immediately . . . Joseph J. Morrison . . . position of claims adjuster . . blah, blah, blah . . .' It's all right here. This is the Claims Department, isn't it?"

"Yes, but . . ." the secretary's brow wrinkled, "was somebody let go?"

Logan threw up his hands and then placed them down amazedly on his hips. "What a jungle. They fire a guy and don't even tell him. Welcome to corporate America."

The secretary had surreptitiously pulled the memo from Logan's hand. She studied it, putting on her glasses.

"This memo isn't signed," she said. "We need something more than this."

Just then, a young messenger entered the office, carrying a thick file holder. This couldn't have worked any better if *I* had hired everyone myself, Logan thought.

"To Mr. Morrison from Records," the boy said.

"That's me, son!" Logan said, heartily. He quickly took the file from the boy's hands. Then he turned, grinning, to the secretary. "You know, I do work so much better sitting down, so if you could just find my office for me . . ."

This was good enough for the messenger; he went back to work. The secretary, however, was still unconvinced. Come on, Logan said, be a little more dim-witted, please, just a little.

"I'll have to see Mr. Philips about this," she said, decisively. "Wait here, please."

With a purposeful look, the secretary disappeared into one of the ominously quiet cubicles. Logan turned to Kelly with a frozen grin.

"Mildred . . ."

"Let's get the hell out of here, Mr. Morrison," she said.

The two of them took it on the run then, their frantic steps resounding not at all on the thick, fancy shag.

If Kelly's office was hardly big enough for the two of them, it certainly had not been meant to accommodate a huge amount of shipping files. As Logan and Kelly went through them that evening, they stacked them everywhere but outside on the ledge. Still, Kelly noticed with amazement, Logan kept them in perfect order.

He pulled another one out and read. "Hong Kong . . . two crates . . . forty by seventy by fifteen . . ."

"London," Kelly read from another, "one crate . . . twenty by eighty by twenty." Kelly tossed it on a pile.

"Mexico City . . ." Logan looked up. "Hey, wait. You tossed the London forms onto the Asian pile."

"That isn't the Asian pile, that's the medium-sized crate pile."

"No, no . . . we're doing this geographically. We're looking for patterns, then for something that radically breaks the pattern."

"I know that, Logan," Kelly said. "But I thought we were doing it by size."

Logan shook his head at her lack of organizing skills. Kelly went back to sorting, ignoring him. Logan grabbed another pile of forms. He read one.

Then he stopped. He stared at it, silently.

"Hello . . ." he said, quietly. "Look at this."

Kelly looked over his shoulder. "From the Taft Gallery to . . . Victor Taft?"

"At a Sutton Place address. But Taft lived on Central Park West."

"And look at the size of the shipment. Bigger than all the others."

Logan nodded. He was beginning to get it. "So Taft sent himself a large shipment at a strange address on the same day we saw that Deardon painting in his gallery."

"The rest of the Deardons?" Kelly wondered.

"Why not . . ."

Logan and Kelly did not bother to put this file in its proper place. They only weaved their way quickly through the rest of them in a mad attempt to get to the door. It would take them a few minutes to reach Sutton Place; they might not have a few minutes.

Kelly's office was not big enough to hold all those files or that many people. But it had been big enough to hold something small and cluttered enough to conceal it.

It was a bug. A secret listening device that had been planted under her desk. It had fed everything they were saying into a cassette recorder, through an earphone, and into the ear of a heavyset man. A man who spent a great deal of his time on street corners, looking into windows. A man who was at that moment seated in a car outside Kelly's building.

The man listened carefully. Then he put down his earphone and picked up the car phone. He dialed the number of someone Logan and Kelly knew.

"I think they found what you're looking for," he said. "But don't worry—you'll get there first."

Chapter Twenty-Five

Logan and Kelly nearly ran up the street from her building to reach Logan's car. They could have easily out-run any other person on their tail. They couldn't out-run a car.

It came shrieking from behind them, with the clear intention of running them down. Logan turned. His eyes wide, he simply pushed Kelly to the right, out of the way, sending her onto the pavement and nearly on her face.

The car's driver had not been prepared for such a tactic; he had obviously intended to hit them and keep on moving. Now he had to contend with a truck coming the other way. He could not contend with it; he and the truck ran right into each other.

The collision was deafening; glass and chrome butted heads; pieces of everything flew everywhere.

Logan turned to Kelly. She was picking herself up and dusting herself off.

"Are you okay?" he asked.

"Are *you* okay?" she asked back.

Logan turned immediately to the accident. The truck driver was angrily straining to get out of the jammed door of his truck's cab. The car driver was quickly exiting his own battered vehicle.

Logan recognized the face. He had seen it outside Chelsea's apartment in Soho.

The man took off then. He weaved his way in and out of frightened pedestrians, occasionally shoving a slow one to the side.

Logan didn't even think. He sprang up and sprinted across the street after him. A cab screeched to a halt, avoiding hitting him by inches. But Logan ran on. Even the sounds of Kelly's concerned cries did not stop him.

Faces blurred to him; he ran with the agility of a halfback, sidestepping, dodging, gaining ground on the heavyset man with every step. People moved to the left and right, as if clearing a path for the big man and the lean blonde man in his pursuit.

Then the man ducked into an alley. Logan reached it and turned into it—only to find that garbage cans had been knocked down, blocking his way. Logan jumped each like a hurdle, not losing much time, watching the man dart out of the light at the other end.

Logan came out of the alley, too, then. He turned—and saw no one. All he saw was evidence of the man's appearance: a street vendor was lying on the sidewalk, rubbing his head after a sudden encounter with him.

Logan looked in all directions. Finally, about a block away on the other side of the street, he saw him. Logan dashed immediately into traffic, bullying his way between cars. Then he ran parallel to the heavyset man, jogging, panting, in the gutter area between the heavy traffic and the thick mass of pedestrians.

He was so close to him; he could have reached out and touched him. The breath came heavy from Logan's mouth; every inch of him ached. Yet he kept running half to help his case, half to salve his pride. He saw the man faltering; he seemed to moan in agony with every step. Soon there were only twenty yards between them, fifteen, ten. Logan just about had him.

Then the man drew a gun. He took a moving shot at Logan, but the lawyer dived right between two scrambling pedestrians, and the bullet missed its mark.

His last resort foiled, the man cut into the street again. But he was no longer fast enough to out-run a car; a cab slammed right into him. There was a sickening thud, and the man was thrown into the air. He came crashing down on the street, twisted in a grotesque position, his head unnaturally bent.

There was a pause. Silence reigned on the street. No one moved. Finally, the door of the cab opened. A traumatized middle-aged man emerged.

"He ran right in front of me!" he shouted to no one, to everyone. "Did you see it? What the hell could I do?"

Logan moved slowly to the body. The crowd closed in behind him, people jostling for a good view of the dead man. Logan knelt. He felt for a pulse; he found none. Then too fast he thought for anyone to see, he slipped the man's wallet from his inside coat pocket. Then he nonchalantly made his way back through the crowd.

Behind him, a short woman watched Logan, suspiciously. As sirens began to be heard in the distance, she raised a finger and pointed it at the man disappearing in the crowd.

"Hey, he took his wallet . . ." she said, quietly. Then she shouted, "Stop that guy! He stole his wallet!"

Logan was moving quickly. Soon he was free of the crowd. He kept walking, kept moving, pretending not to hear.

Then a hand touched his arm.

Logan turned, startled. But it was only Kelly. She was lurching alongside him, trying to drive Logan's own car.

Logan got in. The car bolted spastically forward.

"Nice driving," Logan said.

At a light, Logan and Kelly exchanged places. Logan took the wheel as Kelly rifled through the man's wallet. She found a driver's license, credit cards and other pieces of identification.

"Joe Doe?" Logan asked, still panting.

Kelly shook her head. "Clark. Gary Clark. Hillsdale, New Jersey." She kept searching. Then she stopped. "And look at this—Robert Forrester's phone number."

Logan looked at Kelly. Then they made tracks for what had been their original destination before they were so rudely interrupted: Sutton Place.

Chapter Twenty-Six

It was a beautiful brownstone that dated from the Art Deco era. But that night it seemed anything but pretty; it seemed instead to house the world's ugliest secrets.

Logan and Kelly scanned the names on the mailboxes.

"V. R. Taft . . . ." Logan read. "Three-C."

Kelly sighed. "Most people are lucky to find one apartment in Manhattan. This guy has them all over town."

Logan tried the front door. It was locked. He took out a credit card—one of Clark's—and began to slip it between the latch.

"Something a housebreaker taught you?" Kelly whispered.

Logan was about to reply when the door was opened for him. A stout young man stood there, looking at him, suspiciously.

Kelly thought fast. She grabbed Logan, as if they had been passionately kissing.

"Okay," Kelly murmured to him, "you can come up for a drink, but none of that funny stuff."

"Then what's the point in coming up?" Logan murmured back.

156

Rolling his eyes at the insipid lovers, the man quickly walked past them and out of the building. Kelly caught the door before it closed.

They snaked inside, making sure to close the front door silently behind them. Then they quickly took the stairs to the third floor.

They stopped at Three-C. Both of them were surprised to find the door slightly open. They did not know if it was a trap or a mistake. They only knew they had to go through it.

"I know," Logan said, before Kelly could speak. "We're not breaking, just entering."

They stealthily entered. Once inside, they groped around in the dark for a light switch. Finally, Logan's fingers found one. He switched it.

It was a—what else?—elegant, beautifully appointed living room. It had leather chairs, spotless glass tables, ornate lamps. The only thing it lacked was people. Logan and Kelly went further inside, cautiously.

As they searched, both of them noticed something about the place. While it was beautiful, it lacked any firm decorating scheme, any sense of its having been planned in a style. It seemed perfunctory, impermanent: a lovers' hideaway, not a real home.

Logan crossed to a desk. He shuffled through a pile of bills, an appointment calendar, and various correspondence. He heard Kelly walk into an adjoining room, probably a bedroom. Then he heard her flip a light switch.

There was silence. Then he heard Kelly's whisper.

"Logan. Take a look . . ."

Logan walked over. He peered inside. It was a large, handsome bedroom with huge picture windows. Through them was a generous view of the avenue. A big canopied bed dominated the room, covered by large velvet pillows.

In the corner there were several crates. They were marked Trans-Continental Express.

"Right size for our shipment," Kelly said.

Both Logan and Kelly examined them then. They had already been open. Inside were numerous paintings.

Logan pulled out a small one. He held it up to Kelly. It was a blown up color frame of a soap opera comic strip.

"A minor Lichtenstein," Kelly said. "Probably worth around a hundred thousand."

Kelly continued searching through the paintings as Logan checked around the room. He looked behind the drapes, glanced into the bathroom, tapped walls to search for hollow areas. He stopped then, confused.

"What kind of man leaves a hundred thousand dollar minor Lichtenstein just lying around?"

Kelly was still sorting. "A major Warhol . . . an interesting Dine . . . enough here to fill a small museum . . ."

Logan fixed his eyes on the bed then. He approached it. He sat on it and tested its mattress for springiness. Then he plopped down casually on one side of the endless pile of pillows.

Kelly had stopped looking. "But no Deardons. There's at least two million dollars worth of paintings—but no Deardons."

Logan was thinking. "Try this. We scare the hell out of Taft, so he ships his most valuable paintings from the warehouse over here . . . that way, when he blows up his business records, they won't get torched along with them."

Kelly plopped down into the maze of pillows opposite him. She looked a bit depressed. The feel of the luxurious bed was intoxicating; she snuggled around on it.

"I love huge beds. This should be the smallest size by law."

"Perfect for poor families where the kids have to double up."

Lying there so idly, the two of them had a simultaneous realization: they had never been on a bed together before. Slowly, Logan and Kelly began to recline more. They faced each other, stretched out completely. It was so soft, so comfortable, so secret. For a second, they did not care if someone came in; they even liked the idea of the risk. Kelly rolled over towards Logan then, depressing some pillows, dislodging them.

A bloody hand stuck up in her face.

Kelly screamed. She rolled immediately backwards, shrieking all the way. Logan instinctively jerked the hand away. Then he parted the pillows, dug further into them, revealing a dead body.

It was Robert Forrester's.

Chapter Twenty-Seven

"Jesus Christ!" Logan cried.

He immediately backed off. Then he looked down at himself. His own hand was stained with Forrester's blood. He quickly got up and headed for the bathroom to wash.

He found that he was shaking. He had seen dead bodies before, plenty of them; he had just never been in bed with one, that's all. He ran water into the sink and rubbed his hands vigorously with soap. He looked into the medicine chest mirror and saw that he was pale, practically white.

If Forrester had hired Gary Clark, the hitman, then who had hit Forrester? Logan couldn't see it.

Then he saw something else.

Reflected in the mirror, a dark shadow moved behind the shower curtain. Logan felt his heart beat faster. Yet he kept calmly washing his hands, making no sudden moves.

He called nonchalantly to Kelly. "On second thought, maybe we shouldn't call the police. Maybe we should just . . ."

Logan turned, suddenly. He launched himself against the shower curtain shadow in a flying tackle. He and the mystery man crashed to the shower floor. Logan feverishly pulled away the nylon covering his enemy's face.

It was Chelsea.

"I don't believe this . . ." Logan panted.

Chelsea lay there, dazed, shaking her head, to clear it. Kelly quickly ran in. Her concerned expression changed at once to one of exasperation.

"Not again . . ." she said.

Chelsea was mumbling, absently. "There was . . . a message on my answering machine. A man's voice said to meet you here."

"How did you get in?" Logan asked.

"I have a key," she answered. "This is the place where Victor and I have lived together. I . . . walked into the bedroom, heard sounds from the living room, then hid in there until I could be sure who it was. When I heard Kelly scream . . . I was frightened to death."

Logan helped Chelsea to her feet. He untangled the curtain from around her. Kelly just stood watching, with what still seemed a faint vestige of jealousy. Then the three of them went back into the bedroom.

The minute Chelsea entered the room, her attention went to the bed. Then it went to the bloodied dead man lying upon it.

"Oh, no!" she cried, recoiling.

Kelly ignored the shuddering Chelsea. She went instead to her partner in detection and affection.

"Okay," she said, "let's hear that famous Logan instinct."

Logan shook his head. "You first."

Kelly looked back at Chelsea. She studied her thin arms, her generally winsome shape. "There's no way she could have lifted a two hundred pound man onto the bed. She's innocent."

Logan looked out the window, thinking deeply. His eyes drifted across the street to a park. It was Sutton Square Park. In the center of it was a huge sculpture.

"Wait a minute," Logan said, pointing. "What the hell is that? Where have I seen that before?"

Sniffling, Chelsea joined him at the window. She checked out the large, sloping object.

"The sculpture? It's a Bertolini. It's been there for years."

Logan remembered now. He had leaned on a smaller version of the thing and been admonished.

"We saw the model in Taft's office," he said. "Not for sale because of sentimental reasons, remember?"

Chelsea frowned. "He must have been putting you on. Victor hated that sculpture. He thought Bertolini was a joke."

Kelly and Logan exchanged a curious look. Chelsea smiled, in a nostalgic way.

"We used to lie here at night and look out the window at it and he swore he was going to petition the city to tear it down."

Logan looked at Kelly, Kelly at Logan. They saw the same thought building in each other's eyes.

"We've got to get into the gallery," Logan said. He turned to Chelsea. "What time does it open?"

Chelsea was slightly confused by all the excitement. "It's open tonight. There's a memorial for Victor Taft. What's . . ."

Logan and Kelly started swiftly for the door. Chelsea just followed, as innocent as ever.

Chapter Twenty-Eight

Logan put Kelly and Chelsea into the back of a cab. Then he stood outside and addressed them both.

"I'll be there in a couple of minutes," he promised them. "I'm going to find Cavanaugh. He'll get us a search warrant."

Kelly smiled at him, as if to say, Stickler. Chelsea just gazed at him, smitten. The cab took off.

Logan moved up the block quickly to his car. He got in and started the motor. As he moved his head away for a second from the rear-view, headlights went on in their glass. Across the street, a dark sedan had started its motor, as well.

He drove off, at high speed. The sedan drove, too, but not after Logan. It headed after the cab carrying Kelly and Chelsea.

The two women did not notice their companion. Kelly was too busy wondering about what was to come and worrying about Logan. Chelsea just gazed blankly out the window.

They were still concerned only with their own thoughts when the cab pulled up outside the Taft Gallery. They were already inside when the sedan had come to a full stop.

Rows of chairs had been placed inside the gallery's main exhibition room. Well-dressed members of New York's elite sat politely, some tearfully, listening to eulogies. As one speaker began, they tried to enter as inconspicuously as they could.

"Victor Taft was more than a pivotal force in our thriving art community," he was saying. "He was . . ."

But when it came to the art community—and the Taft Gallery —Chelsea could do nothing inconspicuously. The first sight of her white-blonde hair caused murmurs to start in the audience. Irritated eyes turned, shocked at her presence. The words "How dare she . . ." could be heard more than once.

Chelsea did not hide her face or shed silent tears. Instead she turned a defiant look on the well-heeled horde. Taking her lead, Kelly courageously grabbed a drink from a waiter's tray and downed it in one gulp. Then the two women, basking in their indifference, left the main room.

They made their way to the gallery stairs. Then as quietly as they could, they headed up, several stairs at a time.

Their next stop was Taft's office. Turning on the light, Kelly and Chelsea entered. They did not comb the place, idly; they looked intently for one specific object.

Then they found it.

The model of the Bertolini stood in the corner, as abstract and intriguing as it had always been. Kelly had always admired the thing; now she looked at it as an enemy somehow.

She stepped forward. She rapped nervously and lightly on it with her knuckles. She put her ear closer to it. There was a deep, hollow sound.

She turned to Chelsea. "What do you think?"

"Sounds hollow," Chelsea agreed. "Maybe . . ."

It pained Kelly but she had no choice. She began to twist the Bertolini, to turn it, trying to find some opening. Soon Chelsea helped her, poking around it for a secret button or lever. They were doing that when the man's shadow fell over them both.

Chapter Twenty-Nine

Logan drove as fast as he could.

Kelly and Chelsea were alone at the Taft Gallery—who knew who else would be there and with what aim in mind? His heart raced as he drew closer to the Manhattan South Police Station.

At last, he pulled up outside it. He got out of his car as quickly as possible and ran inside.

In the crowded hallway, he found two detectives standing at a water cooler, smoking and gossiping.

"I'm looking for Cavanaugh," Logan said, intensely.

One of them directed a limp thumb. "In there."

He meant in an office up the hall. Logan practically ran in that direction and didn't slow down until he saw the door marked: "DET. LT. CAVANAUGH."

Logan entered. At first, he saw a typical police office with no sign of habitation. And Cavanaugh was pretty hard to hide. Then he heard a voice.

"Yo!"

From behind him, from a filing cabinet partially hidden by the open door, a lean black man stepped into view.

"I'm looking for Detective Cavanaugh," Logan said, impatiently.

"That's me," the man replied. "What can I do for you?"

Logan felt stunned. He gaped at the man for a minute.

"You're Cavanaugh? You're the only Cavanaugh in Manhattan South?"

The man shrugged. "Unless they've been holding out on me. What's the problem?"

Logan thought he might pass out. Then with grim determination, he regained his equilibrium. He took off from the office without another word.

He ran through the station corridor and out into the street, the realization of his own mistake, the possibility of danger, hammering at his head.

Cavanaugh was a big man, he thought. The kind of man you would want to have on *your* side.

Logan reached his car then. He went through his pockets immediately for his keys. Then he looked up.

"Oh, no . . . Son of a bitch!"

Looking through the closed window, his worst fears were realized: the keys dangled from the ignition.

Logan began to sweat bullets. Cavanaugh was a big man; Kelly was a small woman. He began to wish that Chelsea *had* committed those murders; then she could polish off Cavanaugh. He should only be so lucky.

There was no time for fancy bending and inserting of a wire hanger. Logan looked around for the nearest weapon he could find, something big enough to do some good. Then he found something.

A garbage can.

Logan picked through the thing. He finally came up with an old waffle iron, out of style for some things, but not for others. Swinging it like a tennis racket, he sent it smashing into the side window of his car.

It didn't break.

Grunting now, giving it all he had, Logan directed one more, powerful heave. The window shattered deafeningly into tiny pieces.

The noise brought two uniformed cops running out of Manhattan South. One had a hand on his gun as they swiftly approached the man smashing out the last pieces of glass from his window.

"Hey!" the cop yelled. "What the hell are you doing?"

"Bashing the window out of my car," Logan said, bashing. He gave an exasperated sigh: cops. "I swear to God."

Then he was inside the car. The wind whistling in his face from the broken window, he was on his way to the Taft Gallery.

Chapter Thirty

Kelly and Chelsea both wheeled around, alert to the alien presence. Then Kelly breathed easier. It was Cavanaugh.

She was so relieved to see him; they could use some help *and* some protection. Yet something in the big man's face confused her. He looked angry; he looked more than angry, he looked furious. Cavanaugh had always had flashes of pique—caused by years of resentment, she knew—but this was a different, harsher side to him.

Luckily, it didn't last long. He soon flashed his familiar, reassuring smile.

"Logan's picking up the warrant," he told them. "He's on his way. What are you doing with that thing?"

"Didn't he tell you?" Kelly said. "We think the paintings are somewhere inside that model."

"Is that right? Well, I'll be damned." Cavanaugh gave an admiring grin. "Clever bastard, that Taft . . ."

Cavanaugh was helping them then. He, too, was probing for an opening in the sculpture. But his actions weren't calm and considered; he jabbed and pulled, frenziedly. Kelly began to look at him oddly.

Sweating now, Cavanaugh pulled back, frustrated. A piece of thinning blonde hair had fallen onto his forehead. He seemed altogether crazed. Kelly began to feel afraid. Chelsea instinctively backed off, an animal sensing threat.

"*You're* the cop, Cavanaugh," Kelly said then. "How come *you* didn't get the warrant?"

Cavanaugh smiled. He reached into his pocket, as if to produce it. Then he pulled out a gun, and kept smiling.

"The name's Joe Brock," he said. "Whatever's inside that pile of bones belongs to me."

Kelly caught her breath. She looked at Chelsea, who looked too young to understand. Kelly thought Brock looked pretty good for a man who had died of cancer. Her heart pounding, she wondered how she was going to look deceased.

Cavanaugh-Brock went wild then. He rummaged brutally through a display case in a side of Taft's office. He tested pieces of sculpture for weight; then he selected two that were thick and heavy. He handed one to Kelly, the other to Chelsea. Then he motioned to the Bertolini with his gun.

"Is that the gun you killed Taft and Forrester with?" Kelly asked, boldly.

"It could be the gun that's gonna kill you," he said. "Now go ahead. Take a whack at it."

Kelly hesitated. Logan, she thought, where the hell are you? Then she had no choice but to swing the sculpture in her hands at the model. The impact shook her from head to toe; it actually dented the Bertolini. Cavanaugh motioned for Chelsea to do the same. Obediently, terrified, Chelsea did.

"Swing harder," Cavanaugh commanded. He smiled, maliciously. "Pretend it's my head."

The two women smashed violently at the sculpture then.

"Keep going," Cavanaugh said.

Kelly knew her only hope was to stall. The sculpture was slowly but surely being dented all over; it wouldn't be long now before it cracked altogether.

"Who was the man who shot at us?" she said. "The one who was following Chelsea?"

"He was a nobody," Cavanaugh answered. "A hired hand doing a job. Let's go. Hit it again."

"And when . . ." Kelly panted, between swings, "did you decide to kill Taft?"

"Right after he and Forrester set me up for that prison stretch. I coulda turned state's evidence then, but I decided to wait . . . for *my* turn . . ."

Cavanaugh was beginning to be involved in his memories. Kelly took the opportunity to blindside him with a vicious swing of her sculpture.

Cavanaugh caught the blow just in time, turning so that it only landed on his meaty shoulder. He responded with a withering backhanded slap that knocked Kelly to the floor. Kelly's head hit a table; she sprawled, unconscious.

It was only Cavanaugh and Chelsea then, a mountain of a man and a wisp of a woman. She did not even try to attack; she ran immediately for the door.

Cavanaugh had her then. He grabbed her reedy arm, turned it, and pinned it painfully behind her back. Then he sent her flying into the wall. Chelsea sank limply to the floor.

Cavanaugh went after the sculpture then. Whimpering desperately, he attacked it with his gun butt, hammering at the model with powerful blows.

At last, the thing cracked.

A long metal cannister fell from it, like a dead man. It clattered to the floor. It was big enough to hold many paintings, all rolled up. Cavanaugh bent for it.

Chelsea got there first. Only feigning unconsciousness, ever stronger than she seemed, she reached a pale hand out to grab her father's works. Cavanaugh nipped her effort in the bud; he gripped Chelsea's outstretched arm. Then he clamped a handcuff on her wrist.

Dragging her across the floor, he clamped the other cuff to the leg of a heavy desk. He looked down and grinned at the squirming woman. Then, cannister in hand, he hurried from the office.

Before he could leave the building, he made sure to provide a diversion. He chucked a lighted match into a storage room. He thought Chelsea especially might appreciate that.

Chapter Thirty-One

Logan was stuck.

Fifth Avenue had been completely blocked up due to an accident. Nothing was moving, everyone was leaning on his horn, Logan included. Never try to save someone's life in Manhattan, Logan thought.

But he had no choice; he had to save Kelly; he loved her. And Chelsea, well, she certainly didn't deserve to *die*. Logan suddenly slammed the car in reverse. He pulled backwards and smashed against the front bumper of the car behind him. Then, swinging the wheel hard, he drove out of his lane and did the only thing he could to escape: he drove up on the sidewalk.

Pedestrians scattered at high speeds; he heard shrieks and obscenities. But he barreled ahead, inches away from stores on one side, parking meters on the other. Finally, he saw the accident that had caused all the trouble. He passed it. Then, his tires squealing, he bounced back onto the street.

He drove recklessly all the way to fifty-seventh street. The Taft

Gallery became visible in the distance. But it was not its architecture that was the tip-off, it was something more disturbing: fire.

Flames were darting from the second floor of the fancy building. Sirens were crying out all over the block. Well-dressed mourners were fleeing in droves out of the front door. Many of them were carrying paintings and sculptures under their arms.

Logan felt his heart sink. This could only be the doing of Cavanaugh—or whatever his name was. He just hoped the fire was not set to cover up a murder, or two murders. He had seen that trick used before.

He double-parked his car. He flew from it to the door of the burning gallery. He had to claw his way through the panicked escapees, their terrified faces passing his in a blur.

Once he had reached the entrance, he covered his mouth. The smoke was lethal, the atmosphere suffocating. He waved his way through the black fire clouds, and side-stepped the last of the exiting patrons. The elegant gallery was completely covered by the ugly mist; it seemed to exist now in heaven, or in hell. Logan looked at the stairs.

He saw Cavanaugh. In his mind, Logan gave him no name now. No name but killer.

The big man was carrying a cylinder. Logan did not have to guess what it contained. As soon as he saw Logan, Cavanaugh turned right back around. He started heavily back up the stairs.

Logan was half his weight and twice as angry. He leaped up the stairs two at a time. He reached the second floor just in time to see Cavanaugh disappearing up onto the third.

Then Cavanaugh turned. He had a gun in his hand and he aimed it, haphazardly, still moving. Logan ducked. The bullet took a big chunk out of the wall above his head. He heard more screams of terror from the crowd below him.

Cavanaugh shot again; he missed again. Logan was on his tail, climbing to the third level.

When he reached it, he knew: this was where the fire had begun. The place was ablaze; smoke was billowing out from every room. Paintings had completely peeled from the wall and fallen in ashes to the floor. Sculptures had been scorched and had melted. Logan could barely go on, he was choking so from the smoke. His eyes were awash; his throat was raw. He thought he might gag on the poison.

He could see nothing human. Then he saw something: a shadow, a ghost, moving in the distance. It was too big to be anyone but his enemy.

Logan left his feet. He jumped at Cavanaugh, knocking full tilt into the big man. The two of them went rolling onto the red-hot floor, Cavanaugh's gun clattering away, the cylinder dropping, as well. It was here the two men tusseled.

Cavanaugh was not just hitting him with fists now; he was smacking at him with the broken remains of picture frames. He whacked at Logan again and again, just as he had done the Bertolini. Finally, Logan cracked, too; his hold of Cavanaugh loosened.

The big man tried to push past but Logan's surrender was only temporary. He grabbed hold of Cavanaugh's tree-trunk leg and brought him back down to the floor.

Cavanaugh was clawing backwards at him then, as if trying to peel Logan off of himself. His bent fingers did the trick; Logan was sent reeling.

But he did not stay prone for long. He rose enough to fling a vicious right cross into Cavanaugh's face, sending him stumbling backwards. Logan found his feet. He just kept pummeling and pummeling Cavanaugh, until the larger man dropped.

He fell right into a pile of burning canvases, cracking them beneath him. That was not all he cracked. The floorboards underneath him grunted, groaned and gave way. Cavanaugh screamed.

Logan reached out a hand to him, but it was too late. Cavanaugh fell through the floor to the inferno below. He was a lot of man but it took just a second to eat him alive.

Chapter Thirty-Two

Kelly woke up coughing.

For a minute, she wasn't sure where she was. Had she left the oven on during a midnight meal? Then she blinked a few times and recalled. Cavanaugh wasn't Cavanaugh. Logan wasn't there.

She looked over and saw a troubling sight then. Chelsea was lying on the floor, manacled to a desk. She was wiggling, helplessly. She was nearly choking.

Kelly moved slowly over, regaining her sea legs, brushing smoke from the air. She tried to lift the massive desk to get the handcuff out from under it. It wouldn't budge.

"Chelsea," she pleaded, "you've got to help me. Try to lift it! Come on, goddamit, heave!"

Chelsea rolled over. She made a perfunctory gesture to lift up the desk leg. But it was clear she was too panicked. She stopped trying; then she looked up at Kelly with big, pleading eyes. Just like a puppy, Kelly thought.

"It's no use," Chelsea said. "*You* better get out of here . . ."

"Bullshit," Kelly replied.

Kelly's eyes were beginning to burn. She was coughing in deep, scorching hacks now. She looked around the room. Then her eyes settled on a piece of metal sculpture.

It was long and narrow. Whatever its artist had intended for it, to Kelly it looked exactly like a godsend. She quickly moved towards it and caught it firmly in her grip. Then she wedged the sculpture under the desk, bracing it with a chair. With all the strength in her slight body, she pushed down. The lever action raised the desk by only an inch or so.

Chelsea was struggling, incompetently, unable to pull the handcuffs free. Kelly's entire body ached.

"Come on, dammit!" she cried. "I can't carry this!"

But Chelsea's efforts grew no more efficient. Finally, when it seemed her entire arm would drop off, Kelly desperately kicked the handcuffs loose from under the desk. Then she let the desk slam down heavily on the floor.

Chelsea's eyes fluttered with thanks as she struggled to her feet. Then she stood opposite Kelly, looking helpless.

Come on, Bambi, Kelly thought, pull yourself together. Then she heard a man's voice.

"Kelly!"

It wasn't Cavanaugh's voice, Kelly realized, thrilled. It was Logan's. She turned swiftly around. Sure enough, coming through the door, with a fire extinguisher in one hand, some kind of cylinder in another, was Tom Logan.

He shot a few blasts from the extinguisher in the particularly fiery corners. Then he searched blindly in the office.

"Kelly? Kelly?"

"Logan!" she called back. "Over here!"

He found her then, his waving hand brushing lightly against her face. She caught it and held it there. They looked into each other's eyes, thankfully, saying nothing. Then Logan turned. He saw Chelsea, cowering, shaking slightly, a few tears coming from her eyes.

He did not hesitate. He chucked the cylinder to Kelly. Then he picked up Chelsea and threw her over his shoulder.

"Come on," he said.

As the three of them walked down through the blaze, Logan did not look behind him to check on Kelly. He knew she could take care of herself.

Out on the street, the firemen had to place an oxygen mask on Chelsea, who was gasping a bit for air. She sucked greedily through its nozzle.

Logan looked down at his feet. The extinguisher and the cylinder had both been dropped there. He knelt and picked up the cylinder. Using all his strength, he managed to twist it open. Tipping the thing upside down, he dumped a thick canvas roll out of it.

Chelsea looked up, the sight reviving her as much as the air. Her eyes filled with tears.

"Oh, dear . . . oh, dear. God. . . ."

Kelly gently unrolled the paintings. She and Logan looked at the back of each one. Finally, they handed one to Chelsea, the painting saved from the fire at last, the one inscribed, "To Chelsea, my favorite artist—Sebastian Deardon."

Chapter Thirty-Three

"Your Honor," Blanchard said, "in light of the new evidence defense has presented before this court, the State now recommends all charges against Chelsea Elizabeth Deardon be withdrawn."

It clearly wasn't easy for Blanchard to utter such words. Yet the next morning, with all the new information that had come to light, he had little choice. His chance to get Logan had been foiled. Judge Dawkins banged his gavel.

"The case is dismissed. The court is adjourned."

The courtroom erupted into pandemonium. All the spectators who had come for a juicy trial now seemed satisfied with a happy ending. Chelsea seemed happiest of all. She bathed in the questions and popping flashbulbs of reporters.

Logan and Kelly watched, glad for her. She had known a lot of suffering, Logan thought, and caused a lot of suffering. She had also caused some pleasure, he thought, with a smile. Why shouldn't she now know some pleasure of her own? The defense team started up the aisle.

As they walked, they encountered someone just waiting to say congratulations. District Attorney Maxwell Bower.

Bower was his usual warm but cagey self. The outcome had given him new hope—and an old ambition.

"Congratulations, Tom," he said, with a handshake. "A wonderful job. Comeback of the year."

Logan nodded at Kelly. "I had help."

But Bower did not seem to want to know Kelly that day. Her presence seemed to suggest possibilities Bower wished to avoid.

"Sure, fine job, Miss Kelly," he said, perfunctorily. Then he beamed back at Logan. "We've got a great opportunity here, Tom. All these reporters—all this publicity. This is the time to launch your campaign."

"Campaign," Logan said, blankly.

"For District Attorney, remember?"

"I remember . . . being fired as an *assistant* district attorney."

"Never fired," Bower said, carefully. "Not officially. I never put the paperwork through."

Logan put on a sour smile. Then he turned to Kelly in mock astonishment. "Isn't that amazing?"

"Amazing," Kelly nodded.

"He never put the paperwork through."

"In his own way," she said, sagely, "he was backing you a hundred per cent."

Bower was at great pains to ignore their sarcasm.

"Stop talking like a schoolboy and start thinking like a politician. What do you say? You're the hottest legal property in the city right now. We can win this election just by announcing your candidacy."

Logan stared hard at Bower for a long moment. Let him wonder, he thought. Let him stew for a second. His gaze flickered quickly to Kelly, then back at his old boss. His former boss.

"Forget it," Logan said.

Bower started. Then he tried to conceal his shock. "Too proud to come back?"

Logan shook his head. "Too happy where I am."

With that, he slipped an arm around Kelly. He even let a few fingers stray onto her backside, just for Bower's sake. Then the two of them, Logan and Kelly for the Defense, walked up the aisle.

In the court lobby, they saw Chelsea, surrounded by reporters. She was being barraged by questions and loving every minute of it. Logan and Kelly walked by close enough to check out what she was saying.

"Are you suggesting," one reporter was saying, "that you seduced Victor Taft to get at certain information?"

Chelsea was nodding. Her voice was clear and very cold. "They killed my father. I've watched his body burn for eighteen years. I did what I had to. They were guilty, and they deserve what they got."

Outside on the courthouse steps, Logan and Kelly sat like kids. They let their feet dangle over the edge; they swung their feet to and fro. They felt the light morning breeze play on their faces.

"Vintage Chelsea," Kelly sighed then. "First she slept with Taft, to find out information. Then with you, because she needed your help . . ."

Logan was skeptical. "You think so."

"You don't?"

"Well, at the risk of seeming somewhat immodest, I thought she did it because she was attracted to me."

"We all find you attractive, Logan," Kelly said, sweetly, "And it's perfectly understandable. Chelsea was pretty good at luring men onto beds."

"Extremely good."

"There you go again with the adjectives. Will you please let me pick the adjectives?" She remembered and recited, irritated. "Hypnotic eyes . . . unforgettable eyes . . . okay, she has great eyes!"

Logan looked at her. It wasn't going to be easy, he thought. A new woman, a new job, a new arrangement with his daughter. He was a man who had always let his laundry sit for weeks on end and gotten pleasure from the same old movie again and again. But every case had to be closed sometime. Next case, he thought.

"Not as great as *your* eyes," he said.

A tiny grin spread across Kelly's face. Logan smiled with deep affection. Then they flew into each other's arms. Legal eagles. Lovebirds.

Outstanding Books
On Film
From New York Zoetrope...

American Film Now, Revised Edition. James Monaco. "A cool, thoroughly researched, intelligent, and comprehensive survey of the American film industry... extremely clearheaded and broadly informed." — Larry McMurtry, *Chicago Tribune.*

Cloth. $24.95

Making Ghostbusters: The Complete Annotated Screenplay by Dan Aykroyd and Harold Ramis. Don Shay, ed. This is the exclusive behind-the-scenes story of the making of the most successful film comedy of all time! Over 200 photos and illustrations, including sixteen pages in full color.

Paper, large format. $12.95

Complete Encyclopedia of Television: Series, Pilots, and Specials. Vincent Terrace. Volume I: 1937-1973. Volume II: 1974-1984. Volume III: The Index - Who's Who in Television. Everything you ever wanted to know about American television is included here. Volume I covers almost 5000 entries, Volume II over 3000. Including cast, credits, synopses, network, airdates, running time, and trivia information.

Cloth. Vol. I, II $29.95 each. Vol. III $39.95

The Emerald Forest. Robert Holdstock. Adapted from the screenplay of John Boorman's film, The Emerald Forest tells of a young American boy who one day disappears into the Amazon jungle. A beautifully told story of the confrontation of civilization and mysticism. Includes eight pages of color stills from the film. "A captivating tale." — *Booklist.*

Paper. $7.95

The Art of Heavy Metal: Animation for the Eighties. Carl Macek. Take an exotic, behind-the-scenes tour of the making of the movie Heavy Metal — and the animation business itself.

Paper, 88 color plates. $9.95

These are just a few books about film and television published by New York Zoetrope. To order any of the above, or to receive our free catalogue, write to New York Zoetrope, 80 East 11th Street, New York, NY 10003. Or call toll-free 1-800-CHAPLIN, (212) 420 0590 in New York State.